Sabat 6
The Return

Guy N. Smith

SINISTER
HORROR
COMPANY

PRESENTS

Guy N. Smith

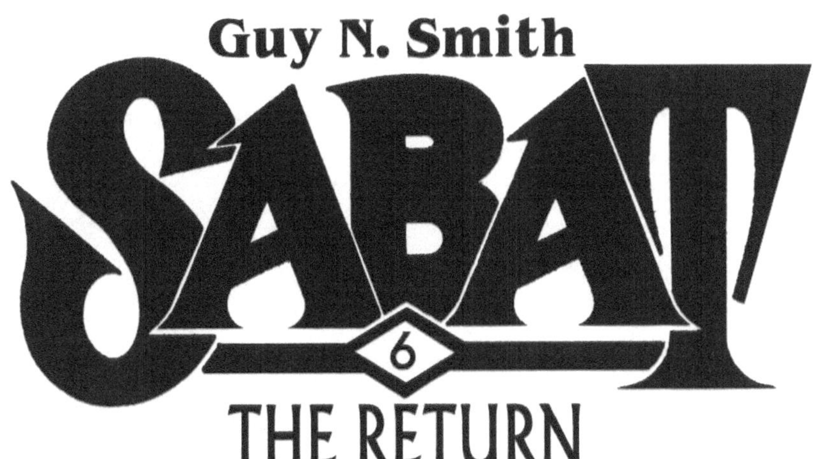

SABAT 6
THE RETURN

Sabat 6: The Return

Copyright © 2019 Guy N. Smith

Edited by J. R. Park
Interior design by J. R. Park
Cover art by Mike McGee

Published by The Sinister Horror Company

SABAT 6: THE RETURN -- 1st ed.
ISBN 978-1-912578-17-7

SinsiterHorrorCompany.com

Other titles in the Sabat series:

Sabat 1: The Graveyard Vultures (1982)

Sabat 2: The Blood Merchants (1982)

Sabat 3: Cannibal Cult (1982)

Sabat 4: The Druid Connection (1983)

Sabat 5: Wistman's Wood (2018)

Prologue

Guy N. Smith

Embraced in a struggle for supremacy the two men splashed and struggled for a foothold on the edge of the raging river, foaming waves threatening to sweep them away.

Mark Sabat, his clothing saturated, his dark hair with flecks of grey plastered over his forehead, as he fought Quentin, his evil brother whose soul had long festered within him. Now the latter had finally materialised into human form and this would surely be their final encounter.

Up above them loomed Wistman's Wood, the most haunted twelve acres of twisted oaks in Britain, a fitting scenario to this long running encounter between good and evil.

'Satan awaits you,' Quentin snarled between gritted teeth, his features depicting his sheer hatred for his adversary.

They slipped on the muddy surface but somehow retained their balance. Quentin was attempting a strangling neck hold on Mark. One hand held him at bay, the other was seeking a devastating blow with a clenched fist. Surely it must end soon, one of them the victor, the other swept away to a watery death.

'This is the end for you, Quentin!' A threat which embodied all the bitterness of the preceding years, ever since their first encounter amidst the zombies of Haiti.

Face to face, Mark grimaced at the foul stench of the other's breath, putrescence from beyond the grave.

On the steep slope above them a woman was screaming, a petite and slender figure with short dark hair, stumbling, falling, picking herself up again.

Toni! Mark was temporarily distracted. His recent partner had no business here, he had ordered her to stay back in her B&B.

Quentin's fist, his arm still grasped by Mark, struck the latter's face. Momentary blackness but somehow he clung to consciousness. He was aware of his foothold slipping, his brother's weight bearing down upon him.

'My master awaits you, Mark!'

Mark was dimly aware of Toni's screams from close by. Somehow she had made it to the edge of the water. He tried to shout to her to keep back, but no words came from him.

Then, suddenly, they both lost their balance, airborne before they crashed into the swirling current. Somehow Mark managed to draw a deep breath and held it before he was submerged. He sensed Quentin's hold on him slackening, breaking free. The raging river took him, he surfaced briefly, took another breath, before he was swept downriver. Swimming was impossible, he had to go wherever the West Dart river took him.

It seemed like he had been hours in the water, surfacing, taking deep breaths before being submerged again. A clump of reeds brushed against him, he grabbed at them but the foliage snapped off, such was the sheer force of the foaming flooded watercourse. Glimpses of high hills, trees, scrubland flashed by.

Surely, eventually, he must be swept to a place where he could grab a hand hold and scramble ashore. A giant wave lifted him, brought him splashing down in the deep water. On and on, tiring. He wondered how much longer his body would stand this ordeal.

Where was Quentin? Had he drowned or had the Dark Powers come to his aid? Would Toni summon help? If so then he must be far from the place where she had last seen him. They would search in vain.

His greatest fear was that of being dashed against rocks which bordered the river, many of them now submerged. The result would undoubtedly be broken bones, maybe unconsciousness, when he would surely drown.

Then suddenly he was brought to an abrupt halt, hitting some partly submerged barrier which was considerably softer than rock. Branches with thick foliage spiked him but did not inflict serious injury. He grabbed a bough; it stemmed his rapid progress downstream. Prickly, but a welcome barrier, a giant conifer which the storm had uprooted and fallen across the river.

Sabat was able to drag himself up into the fallen tree, take some deep breaths and assess his position.

Dusk was already turning to darkness, an adjacent spinney towered above him. He grabbed at another branch and managed to fight his way towards the bank. The current tore at him but there was no way it could whip him from the welcome barrier.

It was a slow and prickly, hard physical fight through Nature's rescue route to the bank where he managed to pull himself up on to firm ground. Exhausted, he crawled away from the floods until he reached the shelter of a conifer spinney. Here he collapsed, thanking his maker for sparing him a watery grave. He lay there in his sodden clothing, unable to move further, and drifted into a deep sleep.

Dawn was breaking when he awoke, somewhat refreshed. He judged that he must be somewhere in the region of Willow Mounds, beyond Two Bridges. So, if he could make his way back along the edge of the flood then surely he must reach Two Bridges eventually. It would be a long arduous trek. He fumbled in his pocket but, as he suspected, his mobile phone was gone, not that it would have been in working order after its soaking.

Up on his feet, he grabbed at a nearby tree for support and waited until his balance returned. Close by the floodwater was creeping further from wherever the riverbank lay. His priority was to avoid a fall.

Yard by yard he progressed, hour after hour. Then, finally, sometime towards midday -- his waterproof wristwatch was still working -- he recognised his destination. Two Bridges was deserted but he saw a single vehicle parked there, his own car. He checked his pocket and gave an audible sigh of relief to discover that his keys were still there.

Soon he was back at his hotel, relaxing in a hot bath. His strength was returning and there were matters to be attended to; the first of which was to go to Toni's B&B in Princetown and reassure her that he was still alive. Then he must contact the police. He wondered how the rescue search had gone on the previous day. How had Quentin fared? Had he also escaped and was free to continue with the evil which he had brought to Wistman's Wood?

'Mrs Anderson is still in bed,' the owner of the property answered his knock on the door. 'She was late returning last night. Apparently a friend of hers had been swept away in the flood and she had stayed there in the hope that he might be found alive. I didn't see her when she came back.'

'I need to see her.'

'First room at the top of the stairs. Maybe I'd better go up and…'

'I'll go up myself,' he pushed past her. 'I'm that missing friend of hers.'

The other stared in astonishment. Perhaps it was best that this stranger went up by himself.

Sabat knocked on the door. A second knocking before he heard movement within followed by bare feet padding on the floor. Like himself, Toni had probably been exhausted and had been sleeping.

A key turned in the lock. The door opened a little way enough to reveal a haggard Toni Anderson, hair awry, holding a dressing gown to her shapely body.

She stared in disbelief, clutched at the door post for support and swayed. Mark stepped forward and held her in case she fainted.

'*Mark!*' she stared in disbelief, perhaps believing that it was a dream sent to plague her tortured mind. 'Mark, I… I don't believe this. The… the rescue party gave up after dark, were certain that you had drowned. I… I…'

He stepped inside, kicked the door closed behind him, pulled her into his arms and kissed her.

'Everything's okay, my darling. It's a long story but right now let's enjoy being together again.'

They relaxed for an hour or so before Sabat eased himself off the bed.

'The police said they'd phone me if they found you,' Toni said, 'but there's been no call.'

'Because they didn't find me,' he smiled. 'But I'm concerned about Quentin, that he may have survived and the evil will begin all over again. I'll borrow your phone and give D.I. Hastings a call. Doubtless they'll be puzzled because my car has disappeared from Two Bridges.'

'Sabat here,' he recognised the D.I's voice.

'Good God, I don't believe it. How the hell did you get out of that flood and where have you been in the meantime?'

'It's a long story which I'll tell you when we meet up. How did the search go?'

'They found a body, smashed to hell on a pile of rocks. Hardly recognizable but it bore a resemblance to yourself. At first they thought it was you. It's in the mortuary now awaiting identification. Maybe you could help.'

'I'll be there shortly.' The hand holding the phone trembled slightly. Doubtless the corpse would be that of Quentin. Dead. Really dead this time?

'Quentin's dead, his body's in the mortuary,' Sabat turned to Toni. 'I'm going over to identify it. Then, perhaps we can live in peace for the rest of our lives.'

The battered and disfigured corpse was undoubtedly that of Quentin Sabat. Mark stared, experienced a sense of sheer relief. After all these years, it was almost unbelievable.

'My brother, Quentin, without a doubt,' he informed DI Hastings. 'Cremation, please, as soon as possible.'

'I'll arrange it,' the officer replied.

Mark attended the short funeral service at the crematorium a few days later. It was a strange experience, watching the coffin disappear into the curtained area. Later the body would be reduced to ashes.

A few days later he collected the urn containing the ashes. He knew only too well what he had to do with it.

He drove to Two Bridges, embarked upon the two mile trek to Wistman's Wood, then made his way down to the river below. By this time the flood had receded somewhat although there was still a strong current.

He unscrewed the urn, tipped the contents into the water and stood watching them disperse as the floodwater carried them away.

That, surely, was the end of his brother.

Later he deposited the empty urn in a convenient litter bin. His feelings were of immense relief.

Toni was waiting for him in her parked car, loaded with suitcases, outside her recent B&B accommodation.

'Well?'

'All done,' he smiled 'Finished. I hope.'

Then they embarked upon the long drive north to Aberdeen. It had been agreed that he would move into her home pending the sale of his own London property. After that?

Well, marriage was a possibility, certainly they would live together in the meantime. Retirement loomed. He promised himself that he would not undertake any more investigations.

He tried to dismiss that old adage that promises are often broken.

1

Guy N. Smith

Toni's house was a neat semi-detached on the outskirts of Aberdeen. For Sabat it was a welcome refuge after living in London.

Her two sons, Joe and Barry, were away at Nottingham university. Her eldest, Edward, was in Edinburgh where he was studying to be a lawyer. Peter, fourteen, was still at school and was delivered by Elsie, her mother, who lived a short distance away,

A grey haired woman of sixty, there was no doubting the suspicion in her stoic expression as she shook hands with Sabat. For her it was something of a shock for her daughter to have gone down to Devon on a biological expedition and then to have returned with a strange man.

Peter bore a remarkable likeness to his mother and was regarding this stranger with undisguised awe. He had been very fond of his late father and right now Sabat was no replacement.

'Well, what are your plans now, Toni?' A forthright

question that demanded an answer.

'No particular plans,' was the reply. 'Mark is moving in with me. We have discussed the possibility of marriage but right now we need to settle after some rather turbulent experiences down south.'

'I see,' Elsie reached for her coat. 'Well, I must be on my way. Call me if you need me.'

'I guess it's all very sudden for her,' Toni switched on the kettle. 'She'll come around to it, though. Right now I'd better get us something to eat and then, Tom, it's off to bed. You've got school tomorrow.'

During the following couple of days the couple lazed around and relaxed.

'I can't believe that Quentin is no more,' Sabat voiced his thought. 'It will take some time getting used to. I keep listening for his vile soul within me but there's nothing there anymore.'

'Well, we're both going to start a new life together.' She kissed him on the cheek. 'You're going to be a happily married man with a young wife and family.'

'It's a lovely thought but it will take some getting used to. I...'

He was interrupted by the loud ringing of the telephone on the hall table.

'I'll get it.' She rushed to answer it, and for some inexplicable reason she experienced a sense of foreboding. Suddenly her entire life had changed.

'Yes, he's right here.' She did not ask the caller's

name, but passed the phone across to Sabat.

'Hello, Sabat, McCaulay here. My word, you took some finding. Got your number from the property agent who's got your place up for sale. What takes you too Aberdeen?'

Sabat hesitated. The last thing he needed was Scotland Yard pestering him. 'McCaulay, you're the last person I expected to hear from. You do know I'm retired, don't you? I'm not taking on any more investigations,' which could only be the reason for the other phoning him.

'Well, it's not quite like that. I really wanted to bring you up to date on rumours that are circulating down here and some information from our undercover chaps.'

'All right, fill me in then.'

'I believe you know G.N. Strong, the private detective who has also retired and is now living in South Shropshire.'

'Yes, I worked with him a year or two ago.'

'Well, do you recall the Reaper, that master criminal, rumoured to have occult connections?'

'I do, but I never had any involvement with him. If my memory serves me right he was caught, got a life sentence, and then escaped from a police escort taking him to another prison.'

'That's correct. But it was G. N. who originally brought about his capture in a shootout, laid him out with a ball stick. It's a miracle the Reaper's skull wasn't cracked! Anyway, at his trial at the Old Bailey he swore revenge on G. N. So we believe, he has now moved up to south Shropshire where G. N. lives in retirement with a dual purpose. He was searching for a missing treasure which had been stolen from a nearby country-house during the English Civil war, hidden in a priest hole at the farm close by and then stolen again. He wanted that treasure and to kill G. N. As it turned out things went wrong for him and he fled before a police manhunt in a neighbouring wood. That's where the mystery begins. G. N. was also with the Armed Support Unit. The Reaper began shooting at them and G. N. dropped him with a shot. When they went to find the body, it wasn't there. Instead a dead wolf lay where it should have been! Explain that if you can.'

'He probably adopted wolf form; it is possible for one with his dark powers. Or else it was an escaped wolf from somewhere prowling the wood and it happened to take G. N.'s bullet instead of the Reaper.'

'Whatever, that's all in the past now,' the Scotland Yard man did not wish to discuss occult possibilities, just hard facts. 'In spite of the massive nationwide manhunt the Reaper escaped from Britain and was believed to be in Paris.'

'Believed to be?'

'Well, he disappeared but was still organising crime from Europe. He is thought to have joined forces with the biggest criminal cartel in Europe known as the "Pink Panther". Their crimes have been huge since 2004 when they stole a 125- carat necklace made up of 116 diamonds from a Tokyo jeweller, worth £20 million. Then came a raid in Mayfair where over £15 million in jewellery was nicked in minutes. There were over 300 other raids in Europe, the Middle East, Asia and the USA totalling £300 million. They are now believed to have their headquarters in Yugoslavia where we have information that the Reaper has been. Until now.'

'So what's all this got to do with me?' Sabat was puzzled, his investigations had only centred on mysteries believed to have some supernatural influences.

'I'm coming to that. As I said, the Reaper has vowed revenge on G. N. and is also seeking the Hatton Hall treasure, both of which will take him to the Bishop's Castle area of South Shropshire. I'm concerned for G. N.'s safety. I have spoken to him to obtain his approval for what I have in mind. Maybe you could go and stay with him for a while. He has now moved into a nearby farm where he has a partner, although he insists she is just a friend whom he protected from the Reaper before that final shoot-out. What do you say, Sabat? Glorious countryside, a kind of holiday. In all probability nothing will happen. I can't arrange an armed guard to protect these folks, there isn't enough evidence to go on, but I'd sleep a lot easier if I knew you were there. After all, there is supposedly an occult connection.'

'Hmm,' Sabat was non-committal. He would not go anywhere without Toni and she had family up here in Aberdeen. They had talked about marriage. 'I'll discuss it with my fiancé and get back to you, McCaulay.'

'Fair enough, I'll look forward to hearing from you, hopefully sooner rather than later.'

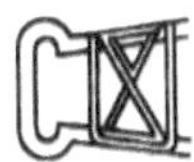

'It depends how long we're going to stay down in South Shropshire,' Toni was not averse to the proposal, but certain arrangements had to be made. 'Joe, Barry and

Edward have their own digs so there's no problem there. It's just Tom that worries me. I'm sure my mother would be only too pleased for him to move in with her and he'd like that because she spoils him. I'll have to talk it over with her. How long are you planning to stay down there?'

'Let's give it two or three weeks,' he replied, 'then if all is peaceful we'll move back up here. I feel I owe McCaulay a favour. There's not enough evidence for him to provide an armed guard for G. N. so I'm his only option.'

'Do you think it'll be dangerous? I still have nightmares about all that happened in Wistman's Wood.'

'Probably nothing will happen,' Sabat tried to sound confident although he had a niggling feeling about the Reaper. 'If the Reaper should show up then I've got a silver bullet waiting for him!'

Toni laughed. 'All right then, I'll go round and discuss it with Mother. See you later.'

2

George Norman Strong was known simply as G. N. amongst his associates. Of medium build, and approaching his 60th birthday, his hair and short beard were black without so much as a fleck of grey. Solely due to his monthly visits to the hairdresser. As he sometimes pointed out to those who remarked upon this, it was not to convince others that he was a somewhat younger man but simply when he viewed his reflection in the bathroom mirror each morning he was not reminded of the passing years. He was fit and agile and it was a way of rejecting signs of age purely for his own determination to continue with his chosen lifestyle in retirement for as long as possible.

From birth he had been destined for a career in banking. Both his father and uncle had been bank managers and they saw it as a safe and socially admired occupation for him after leaving public school. So it might have been, except for his determination to make his own way in life.

Fate had ensured that this would be so. His friendship with a retired police sergeant who had established a business in private detection led to him assisting the latter at evenings and weekends. Then suddenly poor Sam suffered a heart attack and died. There were outstanding investigations that needed to be concluded so G. N. resigned from banking and embarked upon a career in private detection that proved to be highly successful. He assisted Scotland Yard, the Crown Prosecution Service and other organisations from time to time, and was highly regarded on the London scene of criminal investigations

He regarded his capture of the Reaper as the highlight of his career and that was when he decided to retire, purchase a cottage in the wilds of South Shropshire, and pursue his hobbies of collecting and rough shooting.

Amongst his collection of guns was a 9.3 x 82R 16-bore 'Drilling', a 3-barreled combination of a shotgun and rifle. It was with this weapon, an historic collectible from the late 19th Century which was believed to have been in Nazi ownership during World War II, that he had shot at the Reaper on that last manhunt through the wooded hillside close to his home, only to discover that the corpse was not human, but instead that of a wolf.

During this time a somewhat uneasy relationship had developed between himself and the 57 year old attractive widow of nearby Chestnut Farm. He was in love with Parnel Mortimer, a strange experience for himself which he had attempted to conceal from her.

Then he had moved into Chestnut Farm with her somewhat uneasily for both of them. Yet she needed protection, he pointed out, since McCaulay had warned him of the rumours that the Reaper was back in the UK and may well be seeking revenge upon the one responsible for his capture in that police raid in North London.

At least he was now with Parnel. And Mark Sabat and his fiancé, Toni Anderson would be joining them.

At the outset G. N. and Parnel had been sleeping in separate bedrooms. It was up to her, he reflected, to invite him to share hers. Was she just too shy and waiting for him to make the first move? When Sabat and Toni arrived, there would not be a bedroom spare. That would evoke the deciding factor. G. N. licked his dry lips. The decision had to be Parnel's.

'They should be here soon,' he scarcely recognised his own voice.

'I've made their bed up,' she was looking out of the window as she spoke. There was a tremor in her voice.

'Then I'll have to…'

'Yes, move in with me, G. N.'

He slipped an arm around her waist. She turned towards him; head uplifted. Their lips met.

'I've waited a long time for this.' A prolonged kiss, her fingers finding his own and squeezing. 'I guess I'm nervous. Ever since Brian died I couldn't face another man. Until now.'

That was when they heard a car drawing up in the yard.

'Here they are,' G. N. let her disengage herself. Her cheeks were flushed, her eyes sparkled as he had never seen them previously. 'I'll go and let them in.'

'Good to see you, Mark.' A firm handshake. 'A long

time since that investigation at the ruined Bromyard Castle.'

'This is Toni,' more handshakes, 'my future wife.'

'Tea is all ready,' Parnel led the way through to the kitchen. 'You must be starving after that long journey.'

The four of them sat at the table. There was a long silence, each busy with their own thoughts.

'Do you think the Reaper is in this area?' G. N. was the first to speak. 'Or is it just speculation?'

'Special Branch are fairly certain that he is,' Sabat replied. 'According to information gleaned from some of his former UK contacts. If that is the case, then he's almost certain to head up here.'

Another uneasy silence before G. N. asked, 'What's the plan then, Mark?'

'We'll share night watching, G. N. The odds are the Reaper will make his move after dark. We've got to prepare for any eventuality. Last time it was arson but my feeling is that he'll try something different this time. All the same, we'll keep those fire extinguishers handy which you've bought since last time. Smoke detectors?'

'There's one in every room.'

'Excellent. But the Reaper will want you to know that he's killed you, G. N.; watch you suffer. From our point of view that's good because he'll have to show himself and he won't know that I'm here so that puts him at a disadvantage.'

'So we're back to where we were before,' Parnel groaned. 'I…'

A knock on the door interrupted her. They all tensed.

'I'll get it,' Sabat rose to his feet. He gripped the revolver in his pocket, loaded with silver bullets, with one hand, the other held the crucifix around his neck.

'Sorry to bother you.' A uniformed police officer was their unexpected visitor, bearded and with a discerning smile.

'Sergeant Harrison,' he introduced himself. 'May I come inside?'

'Sergeant,' G. N. had followed Sabat to the door. 'Good to see you again. I hope.'

Their visitor was the resident sergeant from Bishop's Castle, well liked in the community, always had a ready smile on his bearded features. Mostly his duties were routine, rowdy youths after the pubs closed, vehicle accidents on the Narrow Roads. He had hoped that those chilling experiences with the Reaper were gone for good. Maybe not.

'Just thought I'd check,' he explained the purpose of his call. 'Doubtless you've been informed that our chaps believe that the Reaper has returned to the UK. If so, then you need to be on the alert at all times.'

'Which is why I'm here,' Sabat nodded. 'Unofficially, of course. There isn't enough evidence of his arrival in this area for the force to employ an armed guard. Also, they're short of officers, having to put extra on the streets in an attempt to combat virtually daily shootings, stabbings and robberies.'

'That's so,' Harrison grimaced. 'There's pressure on us chaps like never before. Even out here we're short on manpower. Anyway, you're aware of the possibility of the Reaper turning up. Right now I can't do any more than warn you.'

'Nice chap,' Sabat remarked as he came back from seeing the sergeant out. 'Well at least the cops are aware of the possible threat. At this stage we can't ask more of them.'

'So, how are we going to organise sentry duty at Chestnut farm?' G. N. looked at Sabat for guidance. 'I guess you're the commanding officer here seeing as the yard requested your involvement.'

'We'll split the night shifts in half, starting as soon as it gets dark. That way we'll each have a chance to catch up on sleep. You can take the first shift tonight, G. N., and we'll change over about 1 a.m. Watch from the upstairs window, changing positions every hour or so.'

'That's fine by me.'

Bess had moved beneath the table and whined softly, just as though in some inexplicable way she remembered the terror from the previous nights of horror.

'Oh, by the way,' Sabat lit a cigarette, 'tomorrow I'd like to have a look up in that priest hole of yours, the one where the treasure had been hidden and the mutilated skeleton of that Roundhead was found.'

'Ugh!' Parnel grimaced. 'It's all been searched by CID. There's nothing left up there.'

'I still need to take a look,' Sabat replied. 'Tomorrow morning?'

'All right,' Parnel agreed with some reluctance, 'but I'll have to call my son, Tom. He lives at Lydham, nearby with his girlfriend, Judy. After the small fire up there he cleared it out and resealed the trapdoor,' she pointed up towards the ceiling. 'I guess he'll have to re-seal it again afterwards.'

'I'm sorry to trouble him, Parnel, but it's an important starting place for myself.'

'Why? What do you expect to find up there?'

'Maybe nothing but evil is renowned for lingering in such places long after unspeakable acts have taken place. Whether it concerns the Reaper or not, I need to know if some force from beyond the grave still exists there. As well as being on guard against an attack from the outside, I have to be sure that something does not exist up there from the previous horrors going back to the civil war.'

Tom arrived towards mid-morning, and there was no mistaking in his cursory greeting that he was somewhat annoyed at having to dismantle his previous work and then afterwards restore the drop-gate in the ceiling over which he had plastered and repainted.

'Just leave me to it. Out of my way. I'll have to leave the cleaning up to you, Mum.'

All four of them vacated the kitchen the two women went through to the lounge, Sabat and G. N. took a stroll around the farmyard.

'I just want to familiarise myself with our immediate surrounds,' Sabat remarked. 'I…'

He was interrupted by a loud shout which came from within the house. Seconds later Tom appeared in the doorway.

Jesus Christ, there's a bloody snake up in the priest hole. I'm not going back up there I can tell you!

'I don't believe it,' G. N. was clearly shocked. 'I've been up there since the fire when it was renovated by the builders. A mouse couldn't get in there.'

'Well, clearly a snake has,' Sabat's eyes narrowed. 'I want to see it. I'll have to get it out somehow. What I need is a net of some kind.'

By this time a somewhat scared Tom had joined them. 'There's one of my old fishing nets in the shed from when I was a kid. I saw it only the other day. I'll go and get it for you, Mister Sabat.'

They entered the house. Parnell and Toni had come through to the kitchen, keeping well back from the open hatch.

'Whatever's going on?' Parnell was both puzzled and clearly frightened. 'I haven't seen an adder on the farm for a long time. Their numbers are in sharp decline in this part of the world.'

'Well, if Tom's correct there's one up in the priest hole and I want to have a good look at it.'

Tom came back into the house, holding a somewhat dusty child's fishing net, cobwebs stringing from it, and handed it to Sabat.

'Thanks,' the other began to mount the somewhat rickety stepladder. A musty smell emanated from up above. He poked his head and shoulders through the square hole and shone his torch all around.

Thick dust adhered to the walls and ceiling, a massive spider crawled into view. Where the hell was that snake?

Then he saw it, curled up in the corner a few feet away. Its head was raised, two tiny eyes watching him, puzzled by the disturbance.

Sabat was familiar with adders, the UK's only venomous snake. He had seen them on moorland when he took relaxing walks. They varied in colours from grey to pale yellow, a dark zig zag marking along the back with a border of spots. A black mark in the shape of an x was visible at the rear of the angular head.

Sabat stiffened. This reptile was almost completely black, the usual markings nearly invisible. He had heard of a melanistic variety sometimes found in Britain but had never seen one before.

He continued to stare, focused the beam of his torch on this reptilian intruder. Usually docile, preferring to avoid contact with humans, this one focused its gaze on him. It had no fear of him, slithering along the rough boards to a massive length approaching 100 cm; a giant of its species. Then it curled up, watching and waiting. For what?

Sabat had heard of adder bites that had proved fatal to ramblers who accidentally trodden on one or poked it and enraged it.

The cane handle of the net in his hand, he inverted the plastic mesh and struck with unerring accuracy. The net opened up, dropped over the snake, its rim firmly on the board floor.

The adder wriggled, squirmed and attempted to free itself. Another flick of Sabat's wrist and the mesh balled, a wriggling mass now clear of the wooden boards.

The handle bowed as Sabat lifted his captive, but held firm. Slowly, carefully, he began to descend a step at a time, and eased his burden through the opening.

Parnel gasped with horror and revulsion, then backed away. She had had a phobia about snakes ever since childhood. Toni stared in disbelief. As a biologist she had encountered virtually every type of reptile in her many searches for plant specimens. She had no fear of them.

'It's a black adder,' she announced. 'Somewhat rare these days. A magnificent specimen, I have to say.'

Sabat stood there and held the netted reptile aloft. 'I'd give anything to know how it got up there.'

'Me, too,' Tom stood in the doorway. 'A very small mouse might have been able to squeeze in from the roof but not a creature that size.'

'What are you going to do with it, Mark?' G. N. spoke for the first time.

'I'd like to set it free,' was the reply, 'but as it has found a way up there previously it could well decide to return.' He gave an involuntary shiver. There was… something about the snake which his highly sensuous powers had picked up. 'I think the safest course for us is to kill it.'

'Adders are protected by law,' Toni's tone was sharp.

'I won't argue with that, but in this case I think we're justified. And who's to know? G. N., perhaps you would kindly fetch one of your shotguns. In the meantime, we'll go outside into the yard.'

Just as though it had heard and understood, the snake began wriggling frantically in an attempt to escape from its mesh prison. All it succeeded in doing was to entangle itself still further.

Tom, Parnel and Toni went back indoors. They had no desire to watch the adder being blasted to a mulch.

Sabat walked to the furthermost end of the farmyard, lowered the struggling captive on to a convenient patch of grass, and with some difficulty shook it free.

G. N. handed Sabat his lightweight 20 bore shotgun. It would do all that was asked of it.

'Thanks,' Sabat turned away, loaded a cartridge into the right-hand barrel and clicked the breech closed.

The shotgun half raised, he swivelled to face his target and that was when his expression registered sheer disbelief. *The net lay flat and empty on the ground but there was no sign of the adder which had been imprisoned within it!*

'This is impossible!' Both men rushed forward and scrutinised that patch of grass on the edge of the muddy yard.

'I don't believe it!' G. N.'s gaze roved all around but there was no sign of that snake. There is no way it could have reached the adjacent buildings in the time it took Sabat to load the shotgun.

'It's completely disappeared!' G. N. wrung his hands together in anguish. 'What the hell's happened to it, Mark?'

'Beyond our ken.' Sabat's expression was grim. 'I've witnessed numerous such mysteries during the course of my career and never found a satisfactory explanation for them. That adder demonstrates to us how fragile our defence against those who follow the left-hand path are. Maybe it was sent to bite us as we slept, to administer death in an agonizing way, the Reaper's revenge on yourself and those who have joined you in the final effort to destroy him. Who knows? We probably never will, but that adder has served a useful purpose for us. It is a warning that the forces of evil are closing in on us. We have to be vigilant every second of both day and night. We have no idea when and where the next attack will come, as surely it will.

3

Hugo Latimer was regarded as the leading expert in skin grafting throughout Europe, possibly in the world. At least that had been his enviable reputation in the medical world until his dismissal for 'improper conduct'. The scandal involved several women who had undergone treatment after which Latimer had taken advantage of their bodies whilst they were still under sedation. Certainly, his removal had been a severe blow to his profession. He was fortunate in that he only received a suspended prison sentence in addition to his dismissal.

Afterwards he left the UK, immigrated to France where he continued to provide treatment, albeit secretly. Wealthy clients were prepared to pay excessive fees for his expertise.

In his late 50s he was somewhat overweight and balding, eyes sunken in a wrinkled, fleshy face. Yet his hands resembled those of a teenager, supple and shapely enabling him to undertake the most intricate skin grafts.

He was well known to the major criminal

organisations throughout Europe and had worked for the Pink Panther cartel on more than one occasion. Such were the facial disguises which he had effected that some of the most wanted men were no longer recognisable from photographs circulated in the press by international authorities.

Soon after the Reaper's arrival in France a meeting was arranged for him with Latimer, taking place in a secret surgery in Paris. Joseph Palmer was about to disappear in the form by which he might have been recognised.

'Tell me,' Latimer leaned back in the chair by the table in his *surgery*, 'what type of characterization do you require, Mister Palmer?'

For one of the few occasions in his notorious career, the Reaper experienced a sense of awe. At some stage he would be rendered unconscious and be at the mercy of another.

'I am looking to become an ageing farmer in semi-retirement, one who has weathered the effects of the elements throughout his previous outdoor life.'

'It can be achieved.' Those beady eyes narrowed. 'But it will not be easy for both of us. It will be painful, for your existing facial flesh will need to be removed before being replaced by a covering of suitable skin. It will need to adapt which will require a period of, shall we say, convalescence. I must add that it will be permanent and its removal could lead to dire consequences for yourself.'

'I am happy to go ahead,' the other was aware of a slight tremor in his voice.

'Then I suggest that we begin at once,' a hesitation, and then, 'needless to say such an operation will be very costly.'

'I am happy to pay. How much?'

'Ten thousand pounds.'

'Then the deal is done. I have the cash.'

'Payment must be in advance.'

Palmer rummaged in a pocket and produced a roll of 50-pound notes which he proceeded to count on the table in the manner of a pack of playing cards. The remainder he returned to his pocket.

'That is excellent,' Latimer shuffled the banknotes together. 'So, if you are agreeable, Mister Palmer, I can begin right away.' He produced a syringe with a long sharp needle. 'Just a prick and then you will be asleep. Leave everything to me.'

The Reaper nodded, closed his eyes, and felt a sharp prick on his left arm. Then he slept, with dreams that his Master was watching him and nodding his approval. Soon he would go in search of vengeance and the missing loot from Hatton hall.

The Reaper stared in virtual disbelief at his reflection in the mirror which Latimer held for him. The skin which covered his face was weather-beaten to a dark brown, cheeks and forehead lined as though with the ravages of passing years. The mouth had been elongated so that dribble oozed from it and the nose reshaped. It had been broken in the process, bulged slightly on one side.

'Excellent, truly excellent,' He scarcely recognised his own voice now a throaty rasp.

'Good,' Latimer replaced the mirror, stood back. 'Now, you will recuperate on the couch in the next room, remain there overnight and hopefully tomorrow you will return to the lodgings where you have lived since your arrival in Paris.'

As he was helped up onto his feet Palmer began to experience pain, a burning, as though his new features were on fire. It was all he could do to prevent himself from crying out. Many times he had inflicted agony on others but had never experienced it himself.

'You will have a burning feeling for some time, hopefully just a few hours,' the other explained, 'but you will have to put up with it. It will recede slowly. Then, hopefully, tomorrow I will organise a car to return you to your lodgings.'

The Reaper lay on the couch in the next room. In addition to his facial discomfort he had a burning thirst.

'It is important that you do not eat or drink,' Latimer shuffled towards the door. 'Hopefully you will go to sleep in due course. There is nothing more I can do for you.'

'It's good to see you back,' the tenant of the small dubious guest house assisted the Reaper up the stairs to the room which he had occupied previously. 'Mon Dieu, I would not have recognised you had not Monsieur Latimer phoned. I have heard reports of his work before, but I would not have believed in their excellence until now.'

'I shall be fine,' Palmer assured him. 'Hopefully in just a few days. In the meantime I want you to contact Leborriou, he is the leader of my European setup now part of the Pink Panther organisation. I shall need a passport to enable me to return to England under the name of Victor Roberts, a retired farmer. Once that is organised and I am back on UK soil, I know what I must do next.'

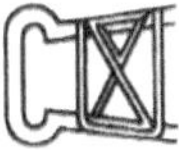

The estate agent in Ludlow could hardly believe his good fortune when a bowed and shuffling Victor Roberts was shown into his office, announcing that he wished to buy a 20 acre smallholding with a dilapidated cottage a couple of miles from Bishop's Castle. 'Willow Field' named after a willow spinney at its rear, had been on the market for over a year. There had been a few casual enquiries but no sales possibly due to the murders which had taken place a year or so ago in the vicinity.

'I want to buy it,' his visitor announced abruptly. 'I have been farming down south and now I am looking for semi-retirement with maybe just a few sheep to look after.'

'Most certainly we can help. At £150,000 I consider it a bargain, although there is a fair amount of work needed on it. I'll take you out for a viewing.'

The dwelling was ramshackle, slates missing off the roof, crumbling stonework and the adjacent field overgrown with gorse and hawthorn.

'It's a deal,' the prospective buyer ignored the

ramshackle house and wilderness. 'How soon can you get the sale through?'

'Pretty soon,' he was assured. 'I know the owner personally. If you would be kind enough to put down a deposit, I will arrange everything with his solicitors. Where are you living at the moment?'

'I'm in a rented caravan just outside Craven Arms. You can have my mobile number to contact me.'

'Would you be agreeable to a deposit of 10 grand?'

'That's fine. I'll get the cash and drop it into you tomorrow.' Palmer thought that producing the money on the spot might arouse suspicions.

Within a fortnight the Reaper had established himself in his new abode. He knew that G. N.'s cottage was only a couple of miles away but first he needed to find out if the missing Hatton Hall treasure was hidden close by. After that...

His elongated mouth dribbled as he smiled to himself. Already plans were materializing in his dark mind. His next move would be to contact an associate in the Pink Panther organisation. This time he would make sure that there were no setbacks. He required reliable assistance in his quest.

4

Both G. N. and Parnel were somewhat uneasy as they climbed into bed. The latter had switched off the light as they undressed and donned their night attire. They lay side by side each facing away from the other. G. N. sensed that she was trembling. Right now sleep was not conducive to the situation.

He wanted to touch her, just squeeze her hand reassuringly. Would it be like this every night for as long as Sabat and Toni stayed with them? After their visitors left would he be returned to the adjoining bedroom?

Silence except for the sound of their breathing. He thought he heard Sabat moving about downstairs, maybe changing his point of vigilance.

Lying on the floor by the bedside was one of G. N.'s other guns, a short barrelled 12 bore hammer gun that had once been a guard's gun on the Union Pacific railway in the late nineteenth century. It was as good now as it had been in those far-off days, a defence against bandits and marauding Indians. Ideal for close range shooting if the occasion arose.

Propped up against the wall was the Drilling. Cartridges for both guns were on the bedside table. He was prepared for any eventuality.

'I'm scared,' Parnel whispered. 'Really scared. Did you notice how Bess was trembling under the kitchen table, like she sensed that something was about to happen? And that awful adder, how on Earth did it get up into the priest hole? And then it just... vanished out in the yard.'

'You're quite safe,' his shaking hand found hers and squeezed it. She made no attempt to resist him. 'We're both here to protect you. If... if anybody tried anything they will be in for a very unpleasant surprise.'

'That, at least, is reassuring.'

He felt her turn on to her side so that she was facing him. He moved towards her. That was when their lips met. Holding hands, they were both trembling. But the time was not right yet, a further move on his part might be disastrous to a relationship which was in its very early stages. *If* it ever materialized.

'I never really got over losing Brian,' she said. 'So sudden. I couldn't bear the thought of another relationship. Until... until now!'

He tensed, squeezed her hand, and then her fingers opened and released him. She moved up against him, breathing heavily.

His shaking hand lifted up the t-shirt she was wearing, then crept upwards until it found a soft breast. The nipple was erect, hard.

G. N. had had virtually no experience with the opposite sex throughout his life. He stroked her, felt her nipple stiffen still further. She was breathing heavily. Her thighs parted, her legs opened wide.

An invitation? His hand slid slowly back down her, finding its way through neatly trimmed pubic hair. Her clitoris was warm and wet. He stroked it and fingered below it; penetrating her.

A gasp of delight came from the mouth against his own, her hand was tugging at him. His erection began, she felt at it, stroking it tenderly, guiding it to where she wanted it.

They shuddered together, suddenly she was desperate for a long-forgotten pleasure, pushing her thighs hard at him seeking an even deeper penetration. The sheets were thrown aside.

For G. N. it was over too quickly, but Parnel was determined to maintain the joining of their bodies until she was shuddering, gasping her delight aloud.

Then they were lying embraced, reluctant to disengage their trembling bodies.

'That was... wonderful,' she breathed. 'Oh, G. N., I've wanted it for so long, but I just dared not. Now... now,' she left whatever she was trying to say unfinished.

'Now... now we're together,' he hardly dared voice his hopes.

'Yes,' she kissed him. 'Really together.'

Slowly they drifted into sleep, the Reaper and the horrors of the past temporarily forgotten.

They were awakened by a knocking on the door.

'G. N.,' Sabat's voice called from the landing. 'Time for your shift.'

G. N. swung out of bed, Parnel's hand clutching at him. 'Sorry my love, but I've got to go. Sentry duty calls.'

He dressed hurriedly, then grabbed the Drilling and some cartridges.

'All quiet,' Sabat assured him. 'Best watch from the landing window. The moon is full so anything that might move out there will be clearly visible. Don't shoot unless it's a definite threat. The last thing we want is to be on a murder charge!'

Sabat went into the adjacent bedroom to join Toni. G. N. moved down to the end window where his companion had already placed a chair. Outside the farmyard was revealed in bright moonlight. Nothing moved.

The coming of daylight seemed an eternity.

'I'd like to have a look around the farm,' Sabat announced after breakfast as Parnell and Toni cleared the table. 'Basically to familiarise myself with my surroundings. We do not know for sure whence any attack will come.'

'Fine by me,' G. N. nodded. 'In fact, I'll take the Drilling. Might bag a rabbit.'

'These days it's always best to have a firearm handy,' Sabat patted his pocket as though to reassure himself that he carried his handgun. 'Right let's go. The girls will be ok for an hour or so.'

Bess was lying on the rug, sleeping. Right now she did not appear to be uneasy and that was a good sign, G. N. reflected.

Up on the steep hillside, sheep were grazing

peacefully. A Buzzard wheeled overhead.

'We'll take a walk through this wood,' G. N. indicated the neighbouring woodland. 'It played a major role in the Reaper's last visit here. Frankly, it gives me the shudders!'

They climbed over the mesh fence, followed the track that led downhill. G. N. pointed out the remnants of the small slate quarry to the left. 'That was where the Reaper and his confederates murdered a guy from the Isle of Man, hid his body and it got eaten by wild beasts. And just up there they killed the gamekeeper. God, this place is a hive of mayhem and murder.'

A few hundred yards further down the track they cut back on to the lower field of Chestnut farm, which would bring them back to their starting place.

Suddenly Sabat stopped, knelt down and examined the rough track.

'What is it, Mark?'

'See those pad prints? Note the four front paw prints and the pad. Look. there are more of them there, made by three creatures travelling together. *Take it from me, G. N., those were made by wolves!* If the tracks were those of a single creature then it would be hunting small prey such as mice and voles. A group means they are hunting larger prey, deer, sheep whatever.'

'Or humans.'

'Not necessarily. Wolves are shy creatures, they will avoid human contact whenever possible. Unless, of course, they are starving.'

'I still can't explain my final contact with the Reaper. He was up on that hillside, armed police and myself below exchanging fire with him. He had singled me out, a couple of bullets came dangerously close, within inches of me. I sited him with this,' G. N. patted the Drilling. 'Went for a headshot. He dropped out of sight. Then, when we reached the place at the top of the hill, it wasn't Palmer who was lying there dead as a doornail, it was a wolf! Explain that if you can, Mark.'

'There could be a perfectly plausible explanation,' Sabat pursed his lips. 'You missed the Reaper but your bullet found a wolf in the nearby undergrowth. Palmer used that as a distraction to make his escape.'

'I suppose it's a possibility. There's a wolf rescue place a few miles from here. They take in old or surplus wolves from zoos and menageries, a kind of club where folks pay to go and observe them. I believe there are occasional escapees. That one I shot could have been one of them.'

'Maybe, maybe not.'

'I've studied wolves in Europe,' Sabat continued. 'Their numbers in the wild are on the increase. And also in the UK. Reports of sightings, though, are few and far between. Just a glimpse by a rambler or similar and they are convinced what they've seen is a German shepherd dog. So we have wolves living in the countryside, more than you think. They hunt after dark, any sheep or deer found dead and eaten are believed to have been killed by dogs or foxes. That's the position these days. These wooded hills are an ideal habitat, there are probably a number of wolves inhabiting them unknown to the locals. Now, having seen these tracks I can assure you that there are at least a trio in the immediate vicinity.'

'I'll take your word for it, Mark. I just hope I don't meet up with them.'

On their way back to the farm a rabbit bolted from a clump of gorse. G. N. bowled it over; the report echoing across the hills.

'Nice shot,' Sabat complimented his companion. 'I guess anybody prowling around the farmyard at night had better look out.'

They both laughed.

5

The Reaper, in his unrecognisable disguise as Victor Roberts had moved into Willow Field. The property was in need of extensive renovation but that was not his concern. If he could locate the missing treasure and exact his revenge upon G. N. then this place could crumble into a ruin as far as he was concerned. By that time he would be far from here. In all probability he would visit Latimer again and undergo a further facial operation. Victor Roberts would vanish as though he had never existed.

First, though, he needed to survey Chestnut Farm after dark, establish that G. N. was living there. He had already checked the latter's cottage, noted that it was empty and that the occupant had moved out, doubtless to the farm. He needed to ascertain if G. N. and Parnel were living there oblivious of his return or whether word had reached them that he was back in the UK and the police had provided an armed guard.

Just as dusk was blending into darkness, Palmer set

out on the long walk through the wood which would take him to Chestnut Farm. His 'cow gown' was fastened around his waist with a length of binder twine. He used a long ash stick to aid the slow and stumbling walk which he had perfected. If anybody saw him then he was the ageing Victor Roberts, a harmless, semi-retired farmer.

In due course he arrived at the top of the sloping hillside which provided an unrestricted view of the Chestnut Farm yard and buildings, bathed in a silvery light from the rising moon. From his pocket he took the night glasses which he had purchased with such surveillance in mind, their powerful lenses giving him a close-up view of the house.

The kitchen curtains had not been closed and within the brightly lit room he saw four people eating a meal at the table. He recognised G. N., sensed sheer hatred for the one who had effected his original arrest and had thwarted his earlier attempt at vengeance. Parnel, too, who owned the small farm. But who were the other two, the dark haired fellow and the younger girl at his side? An armed police guard or simply visitors, maybe relatives? Tomorrow he would pay them a visit, introduce himself as a new neighbour, and find out.

He studied the area below which had once been so familiar to him. Nothing had changed. On the far edge of the yard was a small derelict building in the throes of collapse. Doubtless, it had once been a pigsty.

A sudden thought crossed his mind. Those Roundheads who had hidden the treasure from Hatton Hall up in the priest hole, and then murdered their confederate, might not have taken it too far. They would have probably hidden it somewhere close by for collection later and maybe never returned for it. Where better than a nearby pigsty? It was a long shot but worth investigating. Prior to that he needed to know who those two strangers accompanying G. N. and his partner were. Tomorrow he would pay them a visit.

He set off on a long trek back to Willow Field. He was exhausted. Most of the day had been spent erecting a black altar to his master down in the cellar. Never had he needed Satan's help more than he did now. He had been a faithful servant to the dark powers over the years and surely he would be rewarded for his devotion.

Ricky Brown had recently passed his 18th birthday. A scrawny youth with matted brown hair and a permanent expression of discontent, he had been in trouble with the law on numerous occasions, mostly for petty theft and once for burglary. He had never worked.

He lived with his parents, neither of whom were employed or sought jobs, in a cottage for which their rent was paid by the council. Their income was derived from social security. Nothing was ever likely to change and they were disliked by the local community.

Ricky was short of cash, as usual, and local gossip had fed him an idea where it might be obtained. It was rumoured that an elderly retired farmer had moved into the shambles of a property known as Willow Field. Normally he would have regarded a break-in as a waste of time but, according to local gossip, the old geezer had purchased a van from a local garage and paid with banknotes. So he had plenty of money and was one of the older generation who did not trust banks.

Certainly the place would be worth a look over.

Later that day he trekked out there and, just as darkness was closing in, had knocked on the door. 'Please Mister, I'm lost. Can you tell me the way back to town' or 'could you give me a drink of water?' The latter might just give him admittance to the interior and an opportunity to cast his eyes around.

As it happened, he needed neither for there was no response to his knocking on the door. A van was parked outside so the old guy could not be far away.

Ricky decided to wait; there was nothing to go home for and he did not have enough cash to go to the pub. He settled down by the door. Later he decided that the old man wasn't coming home, at least not yet. Maybe he was visiting neighbours. Breaking in wouldn't take long, a quick search of the room and then he would be away. He donned a pair of polythene gloves so that he would not leave any fingerprints if a police investigation followed.

The lock was old and rickety, and Ricky was inside in less than a minute. He decided to leave the door open; his hearing was acute and he would be warned if the occupier returned.

God, the place stank! Years of being shut up and it was probably infested with vermin. That didn't worry him. He flashed his torch around; a couple of unpacked suitcases by the kitchen table, nothing much else except the remnants of a meal on the table.

His beam picked out a door by the far end. It had to be a cellar entrance for there was no space for a room beyond. It was worth a look, anyway, just the sort of place the old bloke might have hidden any cash.

The door creaked open, somehow held on its loose hinges. Jesus, the stench that drifted up from below had him heaving. So bloody cold, too; goose-pimping his flesh. Then his torch beam picked out a strange and disturbing feature in the corner below; an inverted crucifix above what was some kind of makeshift altar, draped in a black sheet. On the crumbling stone wall above it were chalked a number of strange markings.

Ricky Brown gasped, had to hold on to the rough wall to prevent himself from falling headlong down the steps. It was like something out of those late night horror movies which he watched regularly.

The sooner he was out of this place and away, the better. His legs had weakened, every nerve in his body was shaking. He almost threw up.

And then he heard the outer door creak and slam shut. That old guy had returned!

Well, a doddery senile farmer was no threat to himself. Just push him away and make a bolt for it

He heard a match striking and seconds later the glow from an oil lamp illuminated the scene above. It was the owner, all right, wizened and bent except that the expression on his features belied that of senility, eyes that burned with anger, the mouth agape.

'What are you doing down there, boy?'

'I... I...' Ricky Brown stammered. 'I was... looking for you... I'm lost and...'

'Lost and never to be found alive again!'

The Reaper produced a long, bladed knife from within his tattered attire. The blade glinted ominously in the reflection from the lamp behind. *You have entered the sacred place of the dark powers. You will not leave alive. My master awaits your blood!'*

Ricky lost his footing, fell and rolled down the broken stone steps where he lay upon the filthy floor.

'No, please, let me go, I promise not to tell anybody.'

'Most surely you will never tell anybody!' With strength which belied his frail body the Reaper hauled the other up and sent him sprawling at the foot of the improvised altar.

'*Master,*' his voice was raised, his head bowed in humility, '*I offer up to you this sacrifice, an unbeliever who has dared to infiltrate this unholy place. Please accept his blood as an offering in the hope that you will aid my cause!*'

Ricky Brown's scream died to a gurgle as the razor-sharp blade penetrated his heart. Dripping with blood, it was withdrawn and slashed his throat open. Then it was hacking at the body, ripping the clothing; blood spouting and flowing over the floor.

Only then did the Reaper wipe the blade clean on his victim, stood erect and bowed again.

Now his quest had truly begun, surely his Master would not desert him in his hour of need.

6

The occupants of Chestnut Farm had just finished a late breakfast when they heard a car draw up outside.

'Police,' Sabat half rose and glanced out of the window. 'It's that Sergeant again. I wonder what he wants now.'

'Sorry to bother you,' Sergeant Harrison stepped inside, 'nothing to worry you. No news of the Reaper. It's just that a local youth has gone missing, a teenager named Ricky Brown, got a number of charges against him, theft; burglary etc. Comes from a rubbish family who have reported that he did not return home last night. I've got to make some enquiries but I've no doubt he'll turn up. He's a regular source of trouble and has wasted my time on numerous occasions. I checked with the new owner of Willow Field but he hasn't seen him. In all probability the lad has gone into Shrewsbury or Ludlow and stayed there.'

'Well we certainly haven't seen him,' G. N. replied. 'If we do, we'll let you know at once.'

'By the way, the old guy who's bought Willow Field

was asking about you. He wants to get to know his neighbours and said he might be paying you a visit. He's a bit...decrepit but friendly enough.'

'Then we'll look forward to meeting him,' Sabat smiled. 'As things are at present, the more folks we're in contact with the better. I don't suppose you told him about the Reaper.'

'No point,' Harrison shook his head. 'The Reaper won't be interested in him and I wouldn't want to scare him, doubtless he'll find out in due course about all that's going on in this area.'

Harrison left. Bess wandered out into the yard and seemed to have forgotten her recent unease.

'I was hoping that Tom would come over today and seal that priest hole off again,' Parnel said, 'but apparently he's got a long-distance delivery to make for the haulage firm he works for and may not be here until tomorrow or the day after.'

'That's ideal,' Sabat glanced at the step ladder standing in the corner. 'I think it might be an idea if we did a basic exorcism up there.'

'Oh!' There was undisguised alarm in Parnel's expression. 'I thought that all had been sorted out.'

'It's that adder being up there which concerns me.' Sabat shook his head. 'That and the way it just vanished afterwards. Evil can lurk even after it has been dispersed. I got a strange feeling up there which I can't really explain so I'd feel happier if we did another exorcism. I'll need a bible, a source of salt and a crucifix of some sort, I'd rather keep my own around my neck for the time being.'

'All three are still upstairs where they were left after

G. N. used them. I'll get them for you.'

Sabat re-entered the priest hole and set the exorcism on the floor just beyond the drop gate, closing it after him.

'I can't do any more at the moment,' he announced. 'That should do the trick if evil still lurks up there. Now I think we'll all spend a day relaxing.'

It was a couple of hours later when Bess slunk back into the kitchen, tail between her legs, a low growl in her throat.

'What on earth's the matter with you?' Parnel tensed. The collie's fear had always been a forewarning of danger since those previous terrifying events had begun. What now?

'Somebody just arrived,' Toni came through from the lounge.

Footsteps came down the stairs. Sabat and G. N. who had been resting on their respective beds had also heard. A knocking came on the open door and all four of them moved to answer it.

Bess continued to growl, more loudly now.

Victor Roberts stood there, a hunched figure leaning on his stick for support. His gaze focused on each of them in turn, squinting in the bright sunlight. Saliva dribbled from his thin cracked lips.

'My name's Victor Roberts,' he introduced himself in a faltering voice. 'I recently bought Willow Field, that dilapidated smallholding close to the Bishop's Castle

Road. I thought I ought to call and introduce myself as we're neighbours.'

An outstretched hand was proffered. Sabat was surprised how icy cold it was on such a warm day. A limp grip on each hand in turn before the visitor withdrew it.

Inside the house, Bess was growling beneath the kitchen table.

'Pleased to meet you, Mister Roberts,' Sabat took the lead. 'My name's Mark Sabat, this is my fiancé, Toni Anderson, and George Strong who lives here with Mrs Mortimer.'

An uneasy silence followed. None of them wished to invite their caller indoors and Bess certainly would not welcome him.

The Reaper's gaze moved around his surroundings and settled on the small tumbledown building at the far end, beyond the house.

'Presumably that wreck over there was once a pigsty,' he said. 'Am I right?'

'Yes, it was a pigsty,' Parnel answered him, 'many years ago in my father's day. He bred pigs but it hasn't been used since. In fact, I haven't even looked inside it for ages. We keep meaning to have it demolished and cleared but we never got round to it. That's something I really must ask my son to arrange.'

'Your son lives here, too?' It was a direct question demanding an answer.

'No, he lives with his girlfriend over at Lydham but he comes up here regularly to help me with the farm.'

'I see. Well, a thought has just occurred to me seeing it. I plan to keep a few pigs but there is no suitable outbuildings at Willow Field. If you want to get rid of it maybe I could arrange to have it taken down and the stonework taken over to my place. You would be rid of it and I will have a good start to having a sty built. Just a thought, if I may be so bold.'

'That's an excellent idea,' Parnel saw an instant solution to the problem. 'I'm more than happy to let you have it.'

'Many thanks,' his gaze returned to the old pigsty. 'May I go over and take a closer look at it, just to see what I've let myself in for?' He gave a cracked laugh.

Indoors Bess was still growling.

'Help yourself,' Parnell smiled and added an unenthusiastic invitation, 'then would you care to join us for a cup of tea?'

'No, but thank you all the same. I must be getting back to Willow Field; there is so much to do there.'

The four of them watched him shuffling across the yard and then moved back indoors. Only when the door was closed did Bess stop growling.

The Reaper stood and surveyed the interior of the crumbling building with narrowed eyes. It was one hell of a mess, broken stonework with weeds growing in between, rotten lengths of timber, slates which had collapsed from the roof under the weight of snow over the years.

The earthen floor puzzled him, it was as though it had been raked and forked fairly recently; fresh soil scooped up into numerous heaps. What on earth had been going on in here?

He stooped, saw where there were shallow indentations and what looked like black sausages lying within them. Some had dried out, others were fresh, giving off a faint unpleasant stench. Excreta, deposited by animals. Cats? No, they were too big. Of course, badgers. Brock and his mates had been using this as a convenient toilet on a regular basis.

He used his torch to penetrate the gloom of this dark, windowless place, and swung the beam all around. It was then that something glinted amidst a deposit of foul droppings, catching his eye.

He bent down and used a broken slate to expose it. He stiffened, then let out a gasp of sheer amazement. The object which he had uncovered was a cushion-shaped diamond ring! He probed with a larger fragment of slate and began scraping the hard surface. There was definitely more jewellery buried down there, three more rings and a diamond-shaped emblem of some kind. He trembled with excitement, his shaking fingers scraping them free of dirt.

His hunch had paid off, the thieves had buried the stolen treasure in this convenient nearby location, doubtless for collection later but it had never been retrieved. Possibly they had been killed in an encounter with the King's army and the location of the treasure remained unknown. Until now.

He pocketed the four items and switched off his torch. This was no time to conduct a full search with the occupants of Chestnut Farm in close proximity. It would require a return visit after dark which would not be easy.

A courtesy call at the house brought G. N. to the door. How the Reaper longed to watch his hated foe in the throes of death, screaming for mercy. That would have to wait, though. First he must retrieve the treasure.

'Some of the stonework could prove very useful,' he said. 'I will arrange for somebody to demolish the building and remove anything which can be reused.'

'I would recommend Jack Hadwin, a local contractor who undertakes all types of work. You'll find his telephone number in the directory. Doubtless he will oblige and do the job for you. I know that Parnel will be only too pleased to see the back of that eyesore.'

'Many thanks,' Joseph Palmer, nodded then turned away. 'I will be in touch in a few days.'

As G. N. returned indoors he saw how Bess was cringing beneath the table, shaking and growling.

'What the hell is up with her? Good God, it was only a harmless old farmer.'

'On the face of it,' Sabat was puzzled. 'Animals sense things which are not obvious to us humans. There's evil around, I sensed it just like I used to sense the presence of my evil brother's soul. That adder, for a start, how did he get up there?' He pointed to the drop gates of the priest hole. 'And then just vanish like it had never existed. And that farmer, Roberts, I sensed something odd about him which I can't place. And Bess did, too. I have an uneasy feeling that something nasty is just starting to happen!

7

Shortly after the Reaper's return to his home his mobile phone rang, a series of bleeps which seemed to demand an answer. Hopefully it was the call which he had awaiting. It had to be, nobody else knew how to contact him.

'Roberts.' He used his pseudonym just to be on the safe side.

'Juno Tomic speaking'

Although he was expecting to hear from Tomic he had difficulty in suppressing a groan of annoyance. In recent years his own organisation had combined with that of Pink Panther and although he still occupied a prominent role it was somewhat annoying to have to share it with their leader, Tomic, based in Croatia.

'My confederates will be with you sometime tomorrow night. Obviously they will arrive after nightfall.'

'Excellent. Who are they and where will they be travelling from?'

'They are based in the UK, Bristol. They have been on a job for the Russian government, latterly in Salisbury. But they had to take cover as there is a huge police operation in progress.'

'I see, I think I have heard of it although it is no concern of mine.'

'They are Russians. Their names are Osmakcic and Dimitri. Of course they have adopted UK pseudonyms but that is no concern of yours.'

'I see. As you know I play a leading role in the Panthers.'

'They are well aware of that. They must, however, remain well hidden whilst the three of you formulate a plan.'

'That is no problem. I am an elderly semi-retired farmer, known to my neighbours. Nobody will bother me, I can assure you.'

'That is good. I wish you success with your project.'

The Reaper went through to the dilapidated and untidy kitchen. Right now, he needed something to eat and drink. He reached for a tin of corned beef and a loaf of bread which he had purchased on a recent visit to town. At least the old kettle still worked so he was assured of a hot drink.

His recent visit to Chestnut Farm had proved more productive than he had dared to hope. The missing treasure was undoubtedly buried in that tumbledown pigsty. He gave thanks to those items which had partly exposed it for him, doubtless sent there by his Master in recognition of the recent human sacrifice. That youth had, indeed, been a gift from providence and his short life had not been in vain.

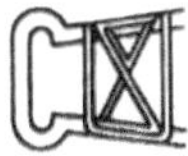

An hour later Joseph Palmer set forth again, this time carrying an old spade which he had found in the outbuilding at the rear of his abode. The Moon was rising, its silvery rays a useful guide to the woodlands track which he must follow.

Caution was a priority once he came in sight of the farm. G. N. and his companion would undoubtedly be watching from one of the windows. He could not afford to be glimpsed.

There was ample cover skirting the farmyard, a thicket of silver birch trees leading to that pigsty. He moved slowly, testing each step before lowering his weight. A cracking of fallen twigs or a dislodged stone could well alert those indoors to his presence. That damned dog would then start growling and barking.

He arrived at the pigsty, eased his way along the crumbling stonework until he arrived at the entrance. Fortunately those trees blocked out the moonlight and provided him with dark shadows which would render him invisible to anybody watching the open yard.

An owl hooted from beyond. Just twice. A sign from his Master that all was well? It had to be, Satan's gratitude for the mutilated corpse sacrificed to him in the cellar of his latest hideout.

Once inside he had no option but to use his torch, a narrow beam shining from a cupped hand. It would not be visible from outside.

He began to dig in the place where he had discovered

those four items of jewellery earlier in the day. The earth was caked hard from many years without exposure to the elements. He used his foot as a lever on the spade for chopping would have created a noise. Excavated soil was piled up beside each hole, carefully examined. Nothing but stones. He cursed beneath his breath and paused frequently to listen. The night was silent, even that owl did not call again.

He was sweating heavily so paused to rest for a few minutes. Maybe there was nothing else buried in here; the thieves had returned to collect their booty but had missed those four items. They in themselves were worth a small fortune so his efforts had not been entirely wasted. G. N. was next on his terrible agenda and then he would be away from here.

Something sparkled in the beam of his torch. Instantly he grabbed for it, rubbed the dirt from it. A diamond bracelet! He began scrabbling in the loosened soil and cast aside small stones. A yellow diamond ring encased in a smaller oval, round diamond, another with pink and purple stones. Still more; four pear-shaped diamonds and three diamond encrusted rings were unearthed.

He scraped out the hole which he had dug but there was nothing more. As he had suspected these were undoubtedly remnants from the main treasure, overlooked by the robbers. Nevertheless it was a small fortune in itself. He deposited them in a pocket of his shabby overcoat. Enough was enough, it was time to leave before his presence was detected.

It was then that a dog began growling and barking from within the farmhouse on the opposite side of the yard.

The Reaper cursed beneath his fetid breath and switched off his torch. His retreat was more hasty than his arrival had been, stumbling on the uneven ground and almost losing his balance in one of the badger scrapings.

Outside he had made it into the spinney before a light shone from an upstairs window of the house. He heard the door opening but by then was out of sight beyond the farm.

That dog was barking furiously now but it made no attempt to follow him. If there was a pursuit he would lose it in the adjacent woodland.

Sabat had the door partly open, his revolver in his hand. He heard G. N. coming down the stairs. Bess had emerged from beneath the kitchen table, growling and trembling.

'What's up?' G. N. had his short-barrelled 12-bore in his hand.

'I'm not sure,' Sabat scanned the moonlit farmyard, 'but Bess senses that something is happening out there.'

'Shall we go and take a look?'

'No, we'll stop right here. If it is the Reaper and some of his gang, we'd be sitting ducks, shot down. Let's wait here and listen, see if we can detect any movements in the shadows.'

'I thought I heard something like a twig cracking as though there was somebody in those trees over by the pigsty.'

Both men fell silent. Behind them Bess still had a low growl in her throat.

'I thought something moved on the edge of the trees.' Sabat had his handgun at the ready. 'Can't be sure though. Keep watching.'

That was when a shape materialized from out of the spinney. Certainly it was no human being, instead it was an animal of some kind. For a second or two it was clearly visible in a patch of moonlight.

'It's a dog,' G. N. muttered.

'No,' Sabat's whisper was tense. 'It's a wolf!'

'Good God, like the one I shot that day when we were exchanging shots with the Reaper!'

Seconds later it disappeared back in the shadows.

'Well, we saw those tracks by the big wood and there was no doubt that they were made by wolves, so this is no real surprise.'

'Too far for a shot with this gun,' G. N. muttered. 'I just wish I had brought the Drilling downstairs.'

'Keep watching,' Sabat ordered. 'If there's one then there's probably more with it. They need not necessarily be anything to do with the Reaper. As I told you earlier, they are living and breeding in Britain, very secretive, usually only hunt at night. When they're glimpsed, folks think that they've seen German Shepherd dogs.'

'What's going on?' Toni and Parnell had appeared at the foot of the stairway.

'Maybe nothing more than hunting wolves,' Sabat whispered. 'Just keep quiet and keep your eyes peeled.'

Bess had joined them, snarling but no way was she going out there.

Outside all was eerily quiet now, no sound of cracking twigs amongst the silver birch, hardly a breath of wind. That wolf had been and gone.

'I'll take over the watch now,' G. N. said. 'The rest of you had better go back to bed.'

Sabat nodded, Toni and Parnel headed for the stairs. Bess had stopped growling and shaking.

'Oh, by the way, Parnel', Sabat closed the door, 'perhaps you would give Tom a ring in the morning, ask him to leave sealing up the priest hole for two or three days. I'd like to leave my exorcism up there for a while longer just to be on the safe side.'

He still had that uneasy, inexplicable, feeling that evil lurked around them. They all needed to be ready for when it materialized in whatever form, as surely it would.

8

It was almost midnight when the Reaper heard a vehicle draw up on the rough ground adjoining Willow Field. The engine died and the doors were quietly opened and shut. Stealthy footsteps scraped on the ground, followed by a tapping on the door.

'Come inside, gentlemen,' Palmer surveyed his two visitors as they entered. Both were of swarthy appearance, caps pulled firmly down on their foreheads. Thick lips parted in a somewhat forced greeting. One was taller than the other, both wore galoshes over their shoes, possibly to deaden their footsteps for there could be no other reason for footwear protection on a dry night.

'My name is Vinko Osamkcic,' the taller of the two uttered a guttural introduction, 'and this is Dimitri. We use pseudonyms in Britain but they do not concern our present mission. We came to Britain some years ago as part of an exchange of spies from Russia.'

'Pleased to meet you,' Palmer nodded. No

handshakes were proffered.

'We have travelled up from Bristol. Previously we were lodging near Salisbury. Now we are far from a huge police manhunt which is taking place there as well as in nearby Amesbury where two of our colleagues have been carrying out a... mission.'

'I have heard about it,' the Reaper smiled, 'but that is of no concern to myself. We have a mission here which we must plan and execute with precision before we are all far from here.'

'We cannot stay here long,' Dimitri spoke for the first time. 'Staying in one place is too much of a risk once we have operated. Two days, three at the most.'

'I'll make some coffee,' Palmer moved to the sink and began filling the kettle. 'Then we must try to formulate a plan.'

'The plan is simple,' Osmakcic slurped his coffee loudly. 'Our method, and we only use one, is to apply a nerve agent to the victim. Novichok is the most effective. We carry two chemicals which must be mixed together a few hours before use. It is safer for us to handle rather than a ready mixed variety. In liquid form it is both colourless and odourless. We make it when an attack is imminent by mixing together two less toxic ingredients. This way it is also easier to sneak it through international borders. Once mixed it is much more dangerous than sarin or VX and harder to identify on the corpse.'

'I see.' For once the Reaper felt uneasy as Osmakcic withdrew a couple of phials from a waterproof pouch. 'Tomorrow night then.'

'No, my friend, *tonight.*'

'But... but how are you going to apply it. The occupants of the house in question have mounted a 24-hour watch. They also have a dog that barks if a stranger is in the vicinity. Further to that I want to watch the man known as G. N. die in agony.'

'It can all be arranged. Now, if you will keep your distance I will mix the toxin in readiness.'

'Just one moment,' the Reaper's tone was terse, 'I want to know more about this nerve agent before we proceed. How will it be used? I want to watch him die in agony and know who has brought about his death.'

Osmakcic let out a loud sigh. He was not accustomed to being questioned. 'In which case, if you insist, then the procedure becomes more complicated. Usually we smear it on something which the intended victim will touch. Death follows a few hours afterwards. It all depends upon which nerve agent is used. Far better to leave the intended victim to die after we have made our withdrawal from the scene.'

'That is not what I want,' the Reaper's cracked lips tightened, there was no mistaking his anger. 'I am paying a considerable sum of money for this and I want it done *my* way. Do you understand? My Master is the Dark One, I have already offered a human sacrifice to him.'

'Our overall master is the Russian government. Orders are relayed from Putin himself.'

'So be it. Then we must work together.'

Osmakcic and Dimitri exchanged glances. they were not accustomed to being queried about their methods.

'Tell me which nerve agent you plan to use, how it works, and its time scale.'

'Very well,' it was Dmitri who replied this time. 'We

have options which we have brought with us.' He produced two small plastic bottles from his pocket along with an object which bore a resemblance to a child's water pistol. 'Novichok 5 and 7 are the most potent. We have both and they need to be mixed prior to use. Precursor chemicals are safer for us to handle than ready mixed nerve agents, colourless and odourless liquid in their pure form. Some Novichok are in powder form and dissolve in water. 10 mg on the skin prove lethal, the victim dying shortly afterwards. They have fits, foaming at the mouth, hallucinating and difficulty in breathing. Anybody coming into direct contact with them will suffer the same fate.'

'Fine, but how will it be applied for maximum effect?'

'Usually on a door handle or some other object which they will be sure to touch.'

'So, if we use that method it entails sneaking up to the farmhouse, applying the agent to the door handle and it probably will not be until the following morning before it is touched. By which time we should have vacated the scene. Apart from that the two men in there are doubtless sharing a 24-hours vigil. Then there is the dog which barks and may well warn them before we have an opportunity to apply the toxin.'

Both assassins were shaking their heads, clearly frustrated.

'Then the only method is this,' Dimitri held up the pistol like appliance. 'See, this works on the principle of discharging a jet of toxin when this lever below is released. Up until then it is kept locked for safety reasons. A jet on target will bring about the results which

I have explained. The victim will writhe for some time before death. If we use this then it will be necessary to kill both men in the house, together with their womenfolk. There must be no witnesses left alive!'

'That sounds fine,' Palmer nodded. 'I am known to them, they will be unsuspecting. So I have to administer the Novichok.'

Lips were pursed. The Russians were not happy about using a third party to carry out the poisoning. Silence lasted several seconds before Osmakcic spoke.

'Very well, you will apply the agent but we shall accompany you. If anything should go wrong our masters would be very angry and doubtless we should suffer the same fate, carried out by other agents in Britain.'

'If you insist upon it tonight then so be it,' the Reaper's agreement embodied a note of reluctance. 'I will make ready and trust upon my Master.'

Osmakcic had prepared the nerve agent, loaded the spraying device and kept it in his pocket. Only when they were close to their destination would he hand it over.

The Reaper had formulated his own plan. On their arrival at Chestnut Farm he would arouse the occupants. They knew him as a neighbouring farmer, they would not be suspicious. He would inform them that he had a problem in that he was feeling unwell. His mobile phone was not working so perhaps they would be kind enough to phone for a doctor. Then he would deliver the deadly spray.

He was not altogether happy with the idea; it had been forced upon him. Nevertheless, it would surely work.

9

Unknown to the Reaper, Osmakcic and Dimitri had formulated their own plans whilst he had been requested to leave the room as they prepared the nerve agent and loaded the spray. They did not believe in supernatural forces only the power which their home country wielded around the globe.

Somewhat foolishly, Palmer had mentioned the treasure which had been hidden for centuries in that dilapidated farm building. A kind of gloating over his previous success. He wished now that it had not slipped out, usually he was secretive but this time euphoria in the first stage of his mission here had loosened his tongue. Not that it mattered, he convinced himself. The Russians were only interested in the project about which they were ready to embark upon.

They stepped outside into the moonlit night. Palmer attempted to lock the door but the lock was broken. He cursed but nobody was likely to enter. That young lad had paid the ultimate price for his attempted burglary.

Carl Carter was a small time poacher. In his late 20s, he was tall and scrawny with a permanent smile on his features. His nose was broken, the result of a fight with the gamekeepers on the estate bordering Willow Field a couple of years ago.

Twice he had been fined for his offences, his firearm certificate has been revoked but he now illegally possessed a .22 Rimfire rifle fitted with a sound moderator. He carried the rifle, stripped down, inside his bulky waterproof coat and these days restricted his forays to the hours of darkness.

He lived in a cottage on the outskirts of Bishop's Castle, his rent paid by social services. His wife had left him, she could no longer tolerate his unreasonable behaviour and those occasions when he flew into a rage and beat her up.

A truly unpleasant character, he survived on his social security payments and money earned from his poaching exploits. He had a contact in the butchery trade who bought his poached rabbits and other game, occasionally a deer if he was lucky enough to encounter one.

Life had been somewhat difficult in the days when there had been gamekeepers on the estate. Then the headkeeper had been murdered and his young assistant had left. He had heard that the syndicate from afar which rented the shooting rights were seeking replacements but right now they had not appointed any.

Which meant that the estate which bordered Chestnut Farm was a safe and easy target for his illegal activities which was where he was headed tonight. He would shoot any fur or feather which presented itself to him on this unprecedented nocturnal foray.

He skirted the old slate quarry. That was where one of the bodies had been hidden. It gave him the shivers which was stupid. All the same he concentrated on the trees directly above it.

The undergrowth rustled as something moved through it. Too big for a rabbit, maybe a deer, a roebuck which would earn him good money. He waited, his back against a tree trunk, rifle at the ready.

The creature pushed its way through a clump of rhododendrons and emerged into a patch of moonlight, clearly visible.

Jesus Christ! He froze, scarcely believing what he saw. It could have been mistaken for a German Shepherd dog at first glance but then he recognised it as a *wolf*. There were wolves in the area, so it was said in the pub. And this was undoubtedly one of them. He dare not risk a shot with his small calibre rifle unless it scented him and attacked. His heart and pulse were pounding; he sweated.

And then it was gone, on through a patch of bracken, heading away from him, doubtless hunting small prey. Phew!

He moved on in the opposite direction. Something fluttered up above him, a pheasant roosting on a branch. No mistake this time. He sighted it, squeezed the trigger and the bird came fluttering down, hitting the ground with a bump.

Kill number one. He stuffed it in a net bag which was hooked over his shoulder. One down and hopefully more to follow. It could be a record night with the entire woodlands at his disposal.

He moved back on to the track above the quarry. Another pheasant; this time he had to search for it in the undergrowth, eventually finding it.

Only then was he aware of three men standing a few yards behind him. One was undoubtedly an ageing farmer, the other two were strangers. He shone the beam of his torch on them. They were staring at him stoically, silently. Threateningly.

'I... I...' for once Carl Carter was lost for words. Who were these strangers in the wood?

The Reaper let out a hiss which embodied his annoyance and anger at coming up on the stranger. Anger because they had been seen and the other could well be a witness to their presence here.

It was Osmakcic who acted instantly, coldly and efficiently. The weapon which resembled a child's water pistol was swiftly drawn from his pocket, aligned at arm's length and the lever pressed with a soft click. A jet of liquid found its mark, sprayed on Carter's features, some of it penetrating the open mouth.

The poacher stumbled backwards and sprawled on the stony path, the rifle dropping from his grasp. He writhed in an instant fit, foaming at the mouth, his breath coming in gasps, mouthing inarticulate barely audible cries.

'Stand back!' Osmakcic ordered his companions. 'Keep well away.'

Carter's arms and legs flayed, growing weaker all the

time.

'Let him die,' the Russians ordered. 'We cannot touch him. We must make a detour around him. Nowhere here is safe.'

The Reaper grimaced, he had not anticipated anything like this.

'If anybody finds him before our mission is completed then there will be a huge police hunt through these woods.' He was disturbed by this latest inconvenience. He struggled to control his rage.

'Whoever finds him will suffer the same fate,' Osmakcic gave a throaty laugh.

'Then…'

'Then we must finish all we have set out to achieve this very night. Give the body a wide berth and continue on our way.'

Reluctantly, Palmer obeyed. He was seething with anger. The signs were not good. He offered up a silent prayer to his Master.

'This package arrived for you this morning,' Parnel handed a sealed cardboard box to Sabat. 'I'm sorry I put it on the shelf whilst you and G. N. were out and about, and forgot it.'

'Ah, excellent,' Sabat produced a penknife and slashed the heavy tape which secured the strong box.

He unwrapped and held up an object which vaguely resembled a miniature telescope with various attachments

'Whatever's that?' G. N. was curious. He never ceased to marvel at the other's surprises.

'Officially it's a FLIR Beach PTQ136,' Mark replied. 'It's a tactical thermal monocular used by law enforcement and military deployment chaps when they are called out at night. In addition to revealing things that would otherwise be hidden by shadows it also reveals the heat given off by living people or creatures. In other words, there's no hiding place for them out there. Technically it's known as a 12um Boson core 1280 x 960 HD display and compact design, so it says on the box.'

'Strewth!' G. N. grunted. 'Now we're really getting technical.'

'This one is handheld,' Sabat continued, 'but they also supply a helmet mounted variety so that the hands are free to use a firearm. It has other features such as on board recording, 7 colour plates for high resolution imagery and a digital compass system inclinometer for situational awareness. I can assure you that nothing out there in the yard at night will be able to approach this house undetected. It's cost me the best part of a couple of grand.'

'Great idea,' G. N. examined the device. 'I take it that we shall share this on our stints of night watching?'

'Most certainly. And I have to say that anybody sneaking around must be shot on sight.'

Parnell paled, Sabat doubtless sensed that the evil was closing in on them.

'I'll maybe shoot me another wolf,' G. N. laughed, attempting to ease the mounting tension.

'Will the Reaper turn out to be another wolf lying

there?'

'As we know there are wolves in the vicinity,' Sabat added 'if we see one in the yard, then we shoot it and we'll see then what we find lying there.'

Only Toni was unfazed. She had every confidence in her lover.

10

The Reaper and his companions made their way up hill in order to skirt the poisoned corpse. It was hard going, a carpet of undergrowth beneath the trees, brambles clutching at their ankles as though in a deliberate attempt to thwart their progress.

Fifty yards further and they began the downward route back to the track below. Osmakcic took the lead, an indication that he was the leader on their murderous trek. The Reaper checked his anger, so long as G. N. died an excruciating death that was all that mattered. Then he would be away with the fortune which he had found in the pigsty.

Suddenly Osmakcic gave a sharp cry of pain, stumbled and fell headlong into a clump of bracken. The Reaper pulled up and flashed his torch. He was just in time to catch a glimpse of a long wriggling shape disappearing.

'Adder,' he grunted aloud.

Dimitri rushed forward, then bent over his prone

companion. 'What is it? What has happened?'

'My ankle!' a breathless grunt of pain from Osmakcic, his leg drawn up, clutching it as he writhed. 'Something... something has stung me.'

'An adder,' Palmer leaned forward, the beam of his torch focused on the Russian's foot as the latter lifted a trouser leg above his ankle. 'He must have trodden on it.'

'Help me... the pain...'

'What do we do?' For once Dimitri did not offer a solution. Reptiles were unknown to him.

'I cannot go to hospital. Must not.'

'Well?'

'Suck the wound, extract the venom, that is the first remedy, and spit it out. If you have a handkerchief, then bind it up as a makeshift bandage.' The Reaper sighed his frustration aloud.

Dimitri grimaced. 'And then we must abandon this mission; try again tomorrow.'

'No!' the Reaper's expression was one of mounting anger. 'We cannot.'

'We must!'

'Very well,' Palmer leaned forward and thrust his face close to that of the other, 'then I must carry out this mission alone. Give me that implement which delivers the nerve agent.'

'I cannot allow...'

'Give it to me now. Then help your companion back to my home. Treat him as I have explained and I will join you later... after G. N. and his companions have writhed in agony and died!'

'All right,' Dimitri rummaged in the pockets of his

thick coat. The Reaper detected the faint clicking of plastic containers. All he needed was the one which fired the jet of Novichok. Why on earth was the Russian carrying a selection?

'Here it is,' He held out his hand, clutching the spray gun. 'As we showed you, depress the lower lever, align the barrel and squeeze the trigger. Move quickly from one to the other of your targets. Once the agent hits them they will not be able to retaliate. They will be writhing helplessly on the ground.'

'Fair enough.' Palmer pocketed his weapon.

'And afterwards the spray container must be disposed of. We will arrange that on your return.'

'Help me,' Osmakcic groaned.

'I will get him back to your house,' Dimitri was clearly powerful as he lifted his companion up on to his feet. 'Use your other leg, the injured one, simply to retain your balance if the need arises. Let us make a start. Progress will be slow. The Reaper may well catch us up if his mission has been successful. Or maybe he will die, too.' he gave a low snigger.

Palmer watched them depart before he moved off in the direction of Chestnut Farm. He experienced a sense of relief; he did not need them now that he had the spray gun. Their presence might have alerted his intended victims.

The deed itself would be akin to opening fire with an automatic pistol and he was a deadly marksman.

It was Sabat's turn to take the first watch. The others had retired for the night and he took up his position by the upstairs landing window which overlooked the yard. The full moon was less bright tonight as it entered its final phase and he welcomed his purchase of the night vision instrument. Through its lenses every detail of the yard and below was clearly visible. There were no shadowed areas by which intruders might sneak up to the house.

His revolver was placed in readiness on the windowsill, the chambers loaded with shells fitted with silver slugs. If the occasion arose he would not hesitate to open fire.

He settled down to wait. It would be a long few hours until G. N. relieved him.

Some time later he heard Bess growling downstairs where she had settled down for the night under the kitchen table. Her growls were interspersed with low barks. What the hell had she sensed now?

He scanned the yard below through his latest acquisition, the shadows vanished as though they had not existed. Suddenly he tensed, a human figure had appeared behind the far barn, bent and shambling.

There was a movement on the landing. The dog had disturbed G. N., he was coming to investigate.

'What's up, Mark? Something has alarmed Bess.'

'There's somebody heading this way across the yard and it looks like old Victor Roberts. Now what the hell is he doing here after dark?'

'Well there's only one way to find out,' G. N. replied.

Both men descended the stairs. Bess had not emerged from under the table. She was clearly disturbed to the point of fear; trembling.

The Reaper knocked the door, stood back with his Novichok weapon partly concealed by his open coat. His finger rested on the release lever. The moment G. N. appeared, hopefully with his companion, a jet of deadly fluid would be directed at them.

The door creaked open, the kitchen light revealed both Sabat and G. N., surprised expressions on their features.

'Why, it's Mister Roberts,' Sabat exclaimed. 'Goodness, what on earth are you doing here at this time of night?'

The Reaper squeezed the tiny trigger on his weapon, shielded from view by his coat. He was expecting a jet of the fluid to hit G. N. before moving on to his companion. Instead there was only a faint, barely audible click. Nothing happened, no stream of death jetted from the barrel.

Fuck those Russians, they had given him an empty weapon, either accidentally or deliberately. He slipped it surreptitiously back into his pocket. Right now he could not risk his intended victims glimpsing it.

'I... I'm sorry to disturb you at this time of night,' his cracked voice trembling slightly. 'you see, I decided upon an exploration of my new surroundings. I intended to be back home long ago. But I got lost. Eventually I saw your farm and I... I wondered if I could get a lift home with you.'

'Of course,' Sabat replied. 'In the meantime come inside and I'll make you a cup of tea.'

Behind them Bess was growling ferociously, but she did not emerge from beneath the table. She was trembling violently. Sabat and G. N. exchanged glances. There was something decidedly odd about this whole business. A harmless old farmer yet...

'Thank you for your kind offer,' Roberts replied, but made no move to enter the house. 'For some reason that dog of yours doesn't like me. I think maybe it would be best if you took me home now, I'm somewhat exhausted, anyway. I have a couple of friends staying with me but they did not wish to accompany me on my ramble. Doubtless they will be concerned because I have not returned. I just hope they haven't gone looking for me and got lost, too.'

'I'll take him back,' Sabat spoke to G. N. 'You stop here and take over my night watch.'

The Reaper cursed inwardly. Alone with G. N. he would have been afforded the opportunity to kill his enemy. Yet it was not to be. Tonight everything was going wrong. Had his Master deserted him in his hour of need?

The Reaper slumped in the passenger seat of the car and pretended to doze out of sheer exhaustion. The last thing he wanted was to engage in conversation with G. N.'s companion.

'Here we are,' Sabat parked outside Willow Field. 'The lights are on and your friends' car is here so obviously they have not gone searching for you. I'll be heading back to Chestnut Farm.'

An actor in every part of his adopted role, the Reaper gave the impression of a frail old man disembarking from the car, grunting with every movement.

'I'm much obliged to you for your kindness,

Mister…'

'Sabat. Mark Sabat. Good night to you, Mister Roberts. Doubtless we shall meet again soon.'

We most certainly will, the Reaper vowed to himself as he made his way indoors, and next time I shall ensure that I do not have an empty container of Novichok.

The Russians were clearly surprised to see him. Osmakcic was lying on the bed, a trouser leg was pulled up to his knee whilst Dimitri was doing his best to treat the snake bite. The wound had swollen, he had sucked it out and was clearly disturbed by his findings.

'Have you got any antiseptic?' he growled.

'No,' the Reaper shook his head. 'Nothing like that. I didn't come here prepared for adder bites.'

'Then we'll just have to hope for the best.' Dimitri began binding the wound with a handkerchief. The patient let out a gasp of pain.

'The spray you gave me was empty!' The Reaper spoke angrily. 'Fortunately they did not glimpse it. We have to try again.'

'Then it will have to be tomorrow night,' was the terse reply. 'I doubt whether Osmakcic will be able to accompany us.'

'Then you and I will have to go. This time with a full container.'

'My apologies for the mistake,' Dimitri averted his gaze, 'but it was dark and I was distracted by that man in the wood.'

Palmer went down into the cellar. He rummaged behind the sacrificial altar and gave a sigh of relief when he found his small treasure trove untouched in a carrier bag. His other concern was that the poacher's corpse lying by the slate quarry might be discovered, but surely nobody would go up there in the meantime.

11

Guy N. Smith

Sergeant Harrison was visited at the police station by Lorna Carter, Carl's ex-wife. Although they had parted, she was clearly just distressed.

'I called around at Carl's,' she stated. 'I sometimes do for we are still good friends. There was no sign of him and his bed had not been slept in.'

'Probably away on a poaching expedition,' Harrison groaned inwardly.

'I know he often poached after dark, but he always returned. Not this time.'

'Maybe he's staying overnight with friends.'

'He hasn't got any. I checked with the neighbours and they haven't seen him. I have phoned the Boar's Head where he usually pops in for a late drink on his way home. There was no sign of him last night. I'm worried that he might have had an accident and be lying out there.'

'Any idea where he might have gone poaching?'

'Undoubtedly on the estate bordering Chestnut

Farm. He told me that they are still waiting to appoint gamekeepers and it's a free-for-all.'

The sergeant sighed. He had no choice but to go and take a look. A bloody waste of his time when he had a load of paperwork on his desk.

'All right, I'll go and take a mooch up there; enquire at some of the small holdings. Leave it with me.'

'I'll ring you later, sergeant.'

Harrison set off, his first call was at Willow Field. Clearly Roberts had visitors, he concluded as he noted two vehicles parked on the rough ground at the front.

'Can I help you?' The Reaper, resembling an aging farmer, answered the door after a lengthy wait. He exaggerated his shaky movements.

Harrison explained the reason for his call.

'No, I haven't seen anybody,' was the throaty reply. 'I've got visitors. We were late going to bed. They're still sleeping off a long journey from down south and I've not long been up and about myself.'

'Sorry to disturb you but I have to check out everybody in the region. There's probably a simple explanation for Carter's disappearance. I'll check out Chestnut Farm next.'

The Reaper tensed. 'I called there last night. I'd been exploring my surrounds and got lost. Mister Sabat brought me home.'

'Thanks, anyway.' Harrison turned away.

The Reaper tensed and watched him depart. Damn all of this, if he found the body up by the old slate quarry the place would be teeming with cops. The planned visit to Chestnut Farm tonight would be severely disrupted. Why wasn't his Master helping him?

It was as though everything had changed with the arrival of Osmakcic and Dimitri.

Sergeant Harrison disliked the woodland route over to Parnel's farm. Those corpses from the time before, the shootout with the master criminal, that wolf lying dead up there, and the Reaper having totally disappeared.

Sometime later after a steep climb he came within sight of the quarry. That was when he saw a pair of booted feet on a narrow path. A body lay sprawled in the undergrowth nearby.

Christ almighty, not again! This had become a place of regular death.

It was Carl Carter all right, the poacher's features were frozen in agony, reflecting the final throes of a painful end, swollen throat still wide from a final scream.

Harrison tensed, then backed away. The clothing on the corpse had been ripped away. Something had been eating the flesh, exposing bloody entrails. Oh God, he almost threw up.

Then he noticed something else lying on the edge of a patch of bracken nearby; an animal with reddish brown fur. A fox. It was dead but the body was contorted, bloodied jaws wide as though it, too, had died in agony.

What the hell had happened here? He shuffled forward with faltering steps and bent over Carter's body.

The sooner he was away from here, the better. He would return to the police station, phone Shrewsbury and summon help. This was a job for the experts, they would know how to deal with it. How had Carter died? At a guess it seemed like some kind of poisoning.

He had almost reached town when he began to feel unwell. His feet were dragging, he almost collapsed. He made it to the office, sank down in the chair by the desk, reached for the phone. He had difficulty in dialling, his hands seemed to be almost devoid of movement.

'Harrison... Bishop's Castle,' he could barely speak. 'Need help... body in wood...'

His voice trailed off, he began foaming at the mouth and had difficulty in breathing. Then came hallucinations; back up there in the wood, lying alongside Carter's mutilated body, trying to squirm away from it. That fox came back to life; was moving towards him slavering jaws wide.

He had lost consciousness by the time the ambulance arrived and paramedics wearing protective gear stretchered him outside

Sabat and G. N. had seen police vehicles and an ambulance passing by on the narrow road beyond the farm.

'Something's happened up there in the wood,' Sabat muttered.

'It's a bad place.' Memories flooded back to G. N. 'A place of death. I wonder who it is this time?'

'Doubtless something to do with the Reaper,' his companion muttered. 'Well, we can only wait and see. Doubtless we shall have callers before long.'

An hour later came the expected rap on the door. The caller was a uniformed police officer who addressed himself as chief inspector Dawson, tall with a clipped moustache and an inscrutable expression.

'There has been a death in the woods up there,' he accepted the seat which was offered, 'by a long disused slate quarry.'

'As there have been others in the past.' G. N. added.

'I am well aware of them,' the officer's tone was sharp. 'This one is somewhat different, though. Our sergeant who discovered it has since been taken seriously ill and is fighting for his life in hospital. Samples from him have been taken and are now on the way to Porton Down laboratory for analysis. The area has been cordoned off. Investigations are in progress.'

'A nerve agent,' Sabat interrupted him, 'like the one at Aylesbury and later at Amesbury?'

'It is too early to say. We must wait until tests have been completed, but the initial signs are that it could be Novichok. Now, where were you two gentlemen between the hours of darkness and midday today?'

'Right here. Apart from a visitor, Mister Roberts from Willow Field. He is a newcomer to the area and whilst exploring the locality, got lost. I took him home.'

'I see,' Dawson's eyes narrowed. 'Were you aware of anybody else in the locality?'

'No, if you care to contact Scotland Yard and speak to inspector McCauley, he will tell you that it is believed that the Reaper is in the locality, bent on revenge upon my colleague here who was responsible for his capture prior to his escape. I was asked to stay here as added protection for my friend. From what you tell me, my own opinion is that the Reaper is responsible for the murder of Carl Carter.'

'Hmm,' Dawson was thoughtful. 'Anyway, we'd better check upon this farmer, Roberts, as he was in the area last night. In the meantime, keep your eyes peeled. Phone the police if you have the slightest suspicion over anything. And, I hasten to add, don't pick up any object which you might find lying about.'

'Well, the plot thickens,' Sabat remarked after Dawson and had left. 'I'd put my money on the Reaper being responsible for this guy's death. If so, it would appear that he was armed with a deadly nerve agent and doubtless on his way here. What stopped him? We must be on our guard night and day.'

The Reaper had seen the police and special medical teams' vehicles heading up towards the big wood. Dimitri had removed their vehicle from Willow Field earlier and parked it in the free car park adjacent to the stockyard in Bishops Castle. It would go unnoticed there as locals used it on a regular basis.

'You two must retire to the cellar below,' he addressed the Russians. An order, his tone brooked no refusal.

'It is a horrible and uncomfortable place,' Dimitri answered.

'That cannot be helped. Undoubtedly the body has been found by now and removed for forensic testing which will prove that Novichok was the cause of death.

There will be a major police investigation. Doubtless they will come here but it will, hopefully, only be a formality. It is unlikely that a frail old farmer would have been the murderer. They will link it to Aylesbury and Amesbury. Tonight will be tricky but we must try. I cannot leave here until my mission is completed.'

With no small amount of reluctance, Dimitri helped Osmakcic off the bed. The latter moved more easily now and did not grunt with pain. They descended down into the cellar and the Reaper closed the door after them. Now all he had to do was await the arrival of the police and give satisfactory answers to their questions.

The expected knock on the door at Willow Field came later that evening. The Reaper exaggerated his shuffling footsteps as he went to answer it.

'May we come inside and talk to you?' The taller of the two plain clothes police officers introduced himself as Superintendent Baschurch. 'And this is Detective Sergeant Wilson,' he indicated his companion, a younger fair-haired man with an air of subservience towards his superior. 'I'm here to inform you that there has been a murder in the wood.' Baschurch did not beat about the bush, 'A local by the name of Carl Carter. We believe he died as a result of coming into contact with a deadly nerve agent.'

'What's that?' The Reaper effected both shock and ignorance in his expression.

'Doubtless you don't keep up with the news,'

Baschurch retorted. 'Nevertheless it can kill in the most terrible manner. We are awaiting a report but in the meantime we assume that it is the one known as Novichok or similar. A local sergeant who found the corpse doubtless came into contact with this substance and is now fighting for his life in hospital.'

'Oh dear.'

'We understand, Mister Roberts, that you were abroad in that wood after dark and that you called at Chestnut Farm. Mister Sabat took you home. He informs me that another vehicle besides your own was parked here but is now gone. You had company then?'

'A couple of associates whom I had not seen for many years were in the area and decided to look me up.'

'Where are they now?'

'They left for London very early this morning. The vehicle was a hired one. They were on their way to holidaying in Spain. They are probably there by now.'

'I must ask you for their names and UK addresses.'

'Ralph Stone and Michael Watson,' the Reaper's reply was instant. 'Their business these days, so they told me, is buying and selling property, hence the reason for their arrival in these parts.'

'So they are out of the country,' Baschurch's suspicions were evident in both his tone of voice and his narrowed eyes. 'I shall need to contact them. Can you supply me with a UK address, phone number or email address?'

'I'm afraid not. They said they would be in touch with me on their return to Britain.'

'I find it rather strange that somebody has visitors without knowing their home address or phone number…' His eyes narrowed.

'I wasn't expecting them. They just turned up and I offered them overnight accommodation to save them the cost of bed and breakfast.'

'Very thoughtful of you,' Baschurch was suspicious, 'yet you left them here whilst you went roaming the hills and woods?'

'They were exhausted. After they had eaten I let them have the only bed in the house. My own alternative was the armchair,' he indicated it in the corner. 'I had no wish to retire so early in the evening, so I decided on a walk.'

'You saw nobody on your ramble?'

'Not a soul. And then I became lost and was most relieved to see Chestnut Farm below me. As I have already told you, Mister Sabat kindly brought me home.'

Baschurch and Wilson looked at each other. The farmer's explanations seem plausible and, anyway, an old guy like Roberts was hardly likely to be carrying a deadly nerve agent? So who had murdered Carl Carter and for what reason? Because he had come upon them in the wood? Why were they there? The Inspector recalled the warning they had received about the possibility of the Reaper being in the vicinity. It all pointed to the latter having killed Carter because the poacher had come upon him. Scotland Yard were concerned that the Master Criminal was seeking revenge on G. N. Strong. It all fitted but at this stage was pure speculation.

'Well, thank you for your help, Mister Roberts,' the police officers turned towards the door. 'I have no doubt that we shall be calling on you again. In the meantime don't attempt to ramble in the countryside. There is already an exclusion zone in place. As soon as we receive verification from Porton Down that Carter died from Novichok poisoning or a similar nerve agent, a warning will be issued to the community not to touch any discarded item. In the meantime, good day to you.'

The Reaper stood behind the closed door, listened to the receding footsteps then heard the car door slam and the engine start up.

He had partly convinced them that he had no part in Carter's death but there was still a lingering suspicion in their minds that he might have had an involvement. Perhaps they'd seen something which he was not telling them.

A faint smile, his disguise had fooled everybody, even G. N. Hugo Latimer had done an excellent job, but he would need to do another when Palmer returned to Paris. Then it would be farewell to Britain. Victor Roberts would disappear as though he had never existed.

First, though, he needed to formulate a plan for the coming night with his Russian confederates.

12

Guy N. Smith

Down below in the stinking cellar, flies swarming on the mutilated corpse of Steve Lewis, the two Russians had listened to the conversation between the Reaper and the two police officers. The night would not be easy, they would have to rely upon their companion to lead them on a route which would avoid the police's 24-hour guarding of the crime scene.

Dimitri had conducted a thorough search of their claustrophobic surrounds. He had found the carrier bag containing the treasure items from the pigsty hidden beneath a pile of rubble in the corner.

'Look,' he showed it to Osmakcic, 'the treasure which the Reaper mentioned. Tens of thousands of pounds worth of jewellery, at a guess.'

'It will be ours after tonight,' his companion whispered.

'True but we need to dispose of him!' He jerked a thumb upwards.

'Then let us send him alone whilst we remain here.

Then we can depart, collect our vehicle and we shall be clear of the country before any alarm is raised. We will give him the weapon; the outcome will be up to him. It is no concern of ours whether or not he exacts his revenge. I will exaggerate the effects of my snake bite. There is no way I can make the long trek. He will have no option but to leave me here and I need you to care for me.'

'Ideal.' They heard the outer door close upstairs. The police officers had obviously departed.

The cellar door was dragged open and the Reaper began to descend the worn steps. 'So far so good. The police have gone. They will doubtless return, possibly tomorrow, but by that time we shall be far from here.'

Osmakcic was sitting with his back against the damp stone wall. His body was twisted in simulated pain, accompanied by loud groans.

'He is not well,' Dimitri announced. 'The wound has worsened. It was all I could do to stop him groaning aloud and giving away our presence to the police. I am afraid there is no way he could accompany us tonight.'

The Reaper grunted 'Then he must remain here and the two of us will go.' His gaze moved to where the treasure was concealed in the corner. The rubble still hid it. He prayed that they had not found it.

'No, I cannot leave him.'

'I cannot go alone, Dimitri.'

'I will not leave my companion. I will give you the spray and you must kill your enemy and his companions yourself. It will be an easy enough task. They will be sprayed before they know what is happening. Then, upon your return, we will all leave.'

'Let's go back upstairs,' the Reaper replied. 'We need to talk this over.'

If the two Russians insisted upon remaining at Willow Field then the Reaper was determined to remove that small bag of civil war loot. He would take it with him, hide it somewhere outside for collection afterwards.

Right now, nothing was going to plan.

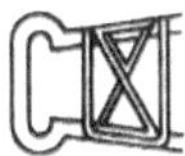

Sabat and G. N., together with their female companions, had just finished their evening meal when they heard a car pull up outside, followed by a knock on the door.

'Police again,' Sabat rose from the table and glanced out of the window. 'I wonder what they want now.'

Their visitor was a young uniformed constable, a ready smile on his tanned features.

'Constable Michael Wilkins,' he introduced himself as he stepped indoors and accepted the offered chair. 'Superintendent Baschurch has decided that, in view of the recent murder and the possibility of a dangerous criminal in the region, you should have an armed guard.'

'That's me,' G. N. stated, 'an armoury of shotguns at my disposal for use if necessary.'

'Fine, but the superintendent feels happier if you had a police guard, at least for the next few days. Can you manage to put me up?'

'If you don't mind sleeping on the couch in the lounge.' There was no mistaking the relief in Parnel's voice at the prospect of additional security.

'G. N. and I have been sharing the night watch,'

Mark smiled. 'It will certainly make it easier for us to have a third guard.'

'I shall be mostly outside in the farm buildings,' Wilkins replied. 'That way hopefully any intruders will be apprehended before they reach the house. It may well be that nothing will happen but at least you will have added protection. I will catch up on sleep during the daytime hours.'

'What's the news, if any, on Sergeant Harrison?' G. N. asked.

'Well, he's very ill but stable. We can only keep our fingers crossed. The Porton Down laboratory have completed their tests and have confirmed that Carter died from Novichok poisoning, a mixture of two types. Harrison came into contact with Carter and consequently suffered the same poisoning although it was lesser than had he been sprayed with the nerve agent. That fox which was scavenging the corpse also suffered the same fate. Now that the corpses have been removed a team wearing protective suits and gas masks are conducting an investigation at that disused slate quarry. A warning is being issued to locals to stay away from that wood.'

'It has all the hallmarks of a Russian murder,' Sabat stated. 'We know that Putin is dumping poison in Britain, yet this would seem to involve the Reaper. The Reaper's organisation is believed to have teamed up with the Pink Panther cartel who operate in Europe and are believed to have their HQ in Croatia. It would now seem that they are using Russian murderers. But that is just my theory at this stage. The Reaper is believed to have occult connections, so between the lot of them we are faced with a very deadly enemy.'

Back at Willow Field, Dimitri, with an exaggerated struggle, had managed to assist Osmakcic up the cellar steps. The Reaper returned below, retrieved the small bag of jewellery and secreted it beneath his coat. No way was he risking leaving it behind.

'I have made up a mixture of the nerve agent,' Dimitri laid the small plastic spray on the table. 'Do not press the lower lever until you are ready to eject it. Then discard it and depart immediately. Even the smallest amount on yourself would prove disastrous. You have three separate ejectors if needed.'

Joseph Palmer nodded. Osmakcic was groaning, clutching at his ankle. It was obvious that there was no way that the latter could make the long trek to Chestnut Farm. In fact, now the Reaper preferred to go alone.

'Before you leave tonight there is the matter of the agreed payment for our involvement,' Dimitri stated. 'Two thousand pounds.'

'You shall have it on my return, I promise you. Not before.'

The Russians glanced at each other. An awkward silence followed.

'We would prefer to be paid now.' In case you do not return. The inference was obvious.

'I do not have the money to hand immediately.'

Another silence.

'Why do you not have it in your possession?'

'Because I will pay you when my mission is satisfactorily completed. It is not in this house so do not waste your time searching for it whilst I am absent.'

Dimitri struggled to contain his anger and frustration. 'So be it then. On your return, I insist that you take us in your vehicle to where ours is parked and then we shall both leave.'

'That is fine. During my absence you must hide down in the cellar. There is always the possibility that the police may return.'

'All right. It is a disgusting, nauseous place, but it will only be for a few hours. Now we must await nightfall. This is one assignment which we shall be relieved to complete and depart from here.'

The Reaper was tense. The hatred which had smouldered within him ever since that night when G. N. had felled him at the shoot-out with armed police in North London was now close to conclusion. The retired private detective and his companions would suffer an agonizing end to their lives before this night was over. It was something to be savoured.

13

Once clear of Willow Field, the Reaper quickened his pace, a mockery of his disguise as a wise and bent aged retired farmer. The waning full moon gave him enough light to see in places, in others he used his stick to detect any obstacle which might cause him to stumble and fall.

He hid the small bag of treasure in the entrance to a convenient badger sett which was easily recognisable. He would return and collect it after he had taken the two Russians to their parked car. Likewise, a consignment of cash was hidden in a dilapidated building at the rear of his home. He would pay them their fee. He could not afford to fall foul of the Pink Panther network. Anyway, the sum was trivial compared with the find of the Roundhead loot.

He turned off the main track some distance from the slate quarry. From here on the going would be more difficult and he could not risk the cracking of branches or brushing of undergrowth. It was a windless night when sounds would carry, and there was a 24-hour police presence in the vicinity. In addition to the nerve agent, he carried his knife and handgun. Tonight nobody would stand in his way.

He trembled slightly; anger. A growing fury as the memory of that night returned, the shoot-out with the cops. The chamber of his handgun had contained only fired shells as he attempted to make his escape. He had G. N. lined up, pressed the trigger but all that happened was a faint click. Then G. N. was upon him and a blow from the other's weighted stick felled him. A spell in prison and then his transfer to Luton, but the prison van was ambushed by his own gang. His escape abroad and later his return to the UK. They were all vivid memories.

Now he was back and the final chapter in his burning desire for revenge on G. N. was only a short time away.

Something moved up above him. He froze, listened, stared. A patch of wan moonlight on the horizon revealed the scrub was being brushed aside. An animal of some species, probably a deer.

Then he caught a glimpse of it. *It was a wolf.* He tensed, then relief as it headed away from him and was lost in the darkness.

More memories flooded back. The last shoot-out above Chestnut Farm. He had G. N. in his sights but ducked to avoid the latter's bullet. It thudded into flesh and fur as a roaming wolf dropped to the shot and saved his life. That was the Master's intervention, allowing him to escape unharmed.

Now another wolf was in the vicinity. Friend or foe? He offered up his thanks to the Dark Powers. They would surely protect him again this night.

He moved on, following a narrow track which led

downhill, and would skirt that quarry. A light showed far to his rear. That would be the police unit which was guarding the place where that guy had died.

Eventually he emerged on to open ground beyond the wood, paused on the summit of this hillside which led down to Chestnut Farm. The farmhouse was in darkness but he knew only too well that G. N. and Sabat would not have retired for the night. One or both of them would be watching from an upstairs window.

This was where the most difficult stage of his quest began. He fingered the nerve agent spray in his pocket and offered up another prayer to the Dark One.

Using hawthorn bushes as cover the Reaper began his descent to the farmyard below.

14

'We can't stop down here in this filthy, stinking cellar for hours until he returns.' Osmakcic sat on the damp stone floor, his back against the wall. 'Especially with *that!*' he nodded towards the mutilated corpse. Swarms of flies were feasting on the open, blood-encrusted wounds.

Dimitri did not reply. Helping his companion back down the crumbling steps had been difficult. Getting him back up would be an even greater problem.

Osmakcic groaned aloud and clutched at his wounded ankle. 'It's starting to hurt again. As bad, if not worse, than before. Burning like it's going septic.'

'There's nothing more I can do. If only we had some antiseptic oil, but there isn't any. Once we get away from here I'm going to find a hospital; get you treated.'

'It could be a giveaway. Get us arrested.'

'No reason why. We are in this country legally and you got the adder bite on a walk in the countryside. We may be Russians but so long as we are far enough away from Salisbury there's no reason why we should be under suspicion. The police will be hunting the other two. We can give our English names, anyway, and we speak the language like we are nationals. There's no reason for anybody to suspect that we came here on an exchange of spies and, even if they did, we've not committed a crime that they can prove. If Palmer doesn't return then we'll have to make it on foot to where our vehicle is parked. I will help you.'

'But we haven't been paid.'

'That is unfortunate, but we cannot do anything about it. The Pink Panther will not be pleased. We can only hope that the Reaper's mission is successful and he returns. Our colleague's mission will keep the police busy in Salisbury.'

Osmakcic began to shiver, his hands trembling. 'It's gone very cold in here, colder than before.'

'You're right,' Dimitri buttoned the collar of the thick coat he was wearing. 'Probably because this place so damp and we can't move about.'

'We could have stayed upstairs no matter what the Reaper ordered.'

'Too risky. If the police should return then it takes time to get you back down here. Also they might hear us.' He lit a cigarette and inhaled deeply.

'I'm in agony,' the other was rubbing his bandaged ankle. 'I can't stand it much longer.'

'I'll go back upstairs, see if by any chance there's some brandy or whisky in one of the cupboards.'

At that moment the dusty light bulb suspended from the ceiling flickered, extinguished for a second or two, then came back on, this time just a dull glow which barely illuminated the cellar.

'It will probably go out altogether,' there was a note of panic in Osmakcic's voice. 'Let's get out of here!'

Now Dimitri was shaking. This underground place was definitely scary and he was not easily frightened. Familiar with corpses throughout his murderous assignments, this one was different, a ghastly sacrificial victim that seemed to be watching them with its dead eyes.

A low groan and it had not come from Osmakcic. At that moment the flickering light bulb went out, plunging the cellar into darkness

Yet even in the pitch blackness they were aware of a shape, a movement in front of the inverted crucifix, a silhouette that was vaguely human in shape; eyes that glowed dull red in a fleshless face.

Osmakcic gave a throaty scream, his companion fell back against him. Who and what was this terrifying apparition that stood before them?

There was no mistaking the sheer evil which emanated from it, an icy coldness and putrefying stench. The whiteness of the skull depicted an open mouth stretched in a snarl.

Osmakcic's feet were scrambling in the rubble of the cracked and broken stone floor. The pain was intense, far worse than when the adder had bitten him.

Dimitri's cigarette fell from his mouth and rolled up against some wastepaper which began to smoulder

That figure before them, no way was it human. The slitted mouth opened and closed, speaking and yet the words vibrated in their brain rather than aloud.

'Traitors! You were sent to kill an enemy of the Reaper but you have instead betrayed him. Now you plan to flee but that will

not happen. Just as this sacrificial victim died, so will you!'

Dimitri tried to rise but it was as though all movement had somehow deserted him. Beneath him Osmakcic was struggling helplessly. There was no way either of them were going to make it up those steps. The flames from the pile of paper had reached the wooden handrail and were travelling up to the open door above.

'I am the Reaper's master. You will pay the ultimate penalty for your treachery!'

Dimitri's brain was in a whirl but survival was uppermost in his rising panic. Who, or what, was this apparition before them? Certainly, it was not human. The handrail was blazing, the fire travelling up towards the room above.

Amidst his panic, a fleeting memory infiltrated his tortured brain. He had given the Reaper one of the loaded Novichok syringes; the other was still in his pocket.

His shaking fingers scrambled, found the pocket, located the plastic pistol-like container. He had difficulty in grasping it, but pulled it clear, fearful that he might drop it. With a grip as firm as he could manage, he located the lever which, when pressed, would emit a jet of the deadly nerve agent and destroy this terrible apparition.

He tried not to meet those burning eyes which focused on him. It mattered not which part of that shadowy shape the jet struck. One drop would be sufficient to send it writhing in agony.

That pile of dry paper in the corner was now alight, flickering flames which were spreading, giving off a cloud of suffocating smoke. It was now or never, his shaking arms raised, he squeezed the ejector lever.

A faint hiss, he heard the liquid strike its target, his aim had been unerring. A hiss came from his intended victim rather than the scream which he had anticipated. That figure should have collapsed in a writhing heap; instead it remained upright, snarling, mocking the one who sought to destroy it.

'Fool, you think you can destroy me! I am impervious to your pathetic attempt. It is you who will die in agony and then you will join my legions in the Flames of Hell, tortured for eternity!'

Dimitri sensed a dampness on his hand, his weapon fell from his grasp. He began to writhe. Beneath him, Osmakcic was jerking, giving off throaty groans of sheer agony. Both were flaying helplessly. The Novichok weapon clicked on the floor but not before its remaining load had jetted over the Russians.

Both were undergoing fits, foaming at their mouths, gasping as they struggled to breathe. Hallucinations blended with the terrible scene before them. Smoke was filling the cellar but that ghastly figure seemed impervious to the choking clouds; mouth wide in a mocking snarl.

'You will both die, slowly in excruciating agony. Then the flames will cremate your corpses, leaving only charred remains to be found. By then your souls will be mine!'

The flames were spreading fast, consuming the thick clothing of the two humans who still writhed in agony at the foot of the cellar steps; then spreading upwards. The ancient wooden door was no barrier to their progress. On into the room above, licking hungrily at the table and chairs, roaring, truly a beast unleashed by the Dark One who stood and watched before departing as inexplicably as he had materialized.

Soon Willow Field farmhouse was ablaze in the night, its roof crumbling as though to bury and hide the dreadful scene which had been enacted within.

An hour later the fire brigade arrived, alerted by the blaze which lit up the hillside above, summoned by the police who were on duty at the scene of the other Novichok murder above Chestnut Farm.

15

The Reaper began the descent of the stony slope, below which lay Chestnut Farm. No light showed from the windows but he had no doubt that G. N. and his companion had mounted a nocturnal vigil. From now on, death was a priority.

This time they would surely be suspicious and see him. No matter, once they were framed in the open doorway a swift jet of Novichok would destroy any threat which they posed to him. As for their female companions, they too, would have to die.

It was preferable to keep to the shadows of the barn and house until he reached the door. Walking nimbly now, with no prospect of being seen, he reached the outbuilding.

And that was when a uniformed police officer wearing a protective jacket stepped out of the darkness in front of him.

'Hold it right there!' Michael Wilkes had rested on his holstered handgun.

The Reaper started and almost lost his footing.

'What the...'

'And who might you be and what are you doing creeping around here at this time of night?' Wilkes was clearly suspicious even though he was faced with a frail old man. One never underestimated anybody when criminals were at large.

'I... I, my name is Roberts. I'm a neighbouring farmer.'

'What are you doing here?'

'I... I,' for once the other was taken by surprise. 'I'm new to this area. I had been exploring and got lost. I know Mister Strong and I was... going to ask if he would take me home.' The same excuse which he had used previously but this copper would not know that.

'Then I'd better accompany you to the house. They are probably all in bed. Except whoever is on Night Watch.'

Behind them the sky was suddenly lit up by an orange blaze which could only have come from a fire somewhere nearby.

'Look there's a blaze over there, probably a hill fire. The undergrowth is very dry.' The Reaper diverted the attention of the other. He knew only too well what he must do. This copper had to be silenced before he raised the alarm.

He had a trio of choices. The Novichock might result in screams as his intended victim writhed in agony, the handgun was too noisy, which left only the sharp bladed knife in his coat.

'I'd better go to the house and phone the fire brigade,' Wilkes grunted. 'There's no mobile signal up here, and for some reason my radio doesn't appear to be working.'

The policeman turned away and that was when the Reaper struck, his 6-inch honed blade burying itself in the side of the officer's neck.

Wilkes grunted, stumbled and fell, blood gushing from the deep wound. The Reaper withdrew the dripping blade and struck again. His victim gurgled, arms moving weakly and then lay still.

Joseph Palmer let out a loud sigh, wiped the knife blade clean on his victim's uniform and returned it to its sheath. He had not bargained on the occupants of Chestnut Farm having a police guard. No matter, that problem was solved.

Now for G. N. and the others. He eased his way along the outbuildings. Somewhere behind him he heard a long drawn out howl.

Wolves! Had his master dispatched a wolven army to assist him should all else fail? Like the time when that beast had taken the bullet intended for himself at the shoot-out with the police. He felt somewhat easier at the thought. Tonight G. N. was definitely going to die.

Sabat had taken the first watch at the farm. He tested his thermal monocular and was amazed at the details which were exposed in areas of total darkness. On the hillside opposite it revealed a hunting fox which otherwise would have been invisible to the naked eye through standard magnification night lenses.

Something else moved up beyond the fox. A brief glimpse as they crossed a small patch of open ground before disappearing into thick gorse. Sabat caught his breath. *Wolves, there was no doubt about it. Three, maybe four of them, and heading in this direction!*

Then he detected another movement down at the far end of the farmyard. He focused on it. A human shape. PC Wilkes of course. Doubtless the officer was embarking upon a short patrol. It had to be exceedingly boring stationed inside a sheep barn for hours on end. Now the other was lost to view behind the end building. No problem there. Chestnut Farm certainly had watertight security at present.

Time passed. There were no further signs of Wilkes, he had even gone further afield or else returned to his post when Sabat was not looking.

'All quiet out there?' G. N. appeared at the end of the landing, his Drilling cradled beneath his arm. It was time to relieve his companion.

'Seems to be. Wilkes appears to have gone on a patrol beyond the farmyard. Then I glimpsed some wolves up on the hillside, heading in this direction. More than one indicates that they are hunting large prey. Possibly deer. Anyway, we can forget them. I hope! At least Wilkes is armed. I still get that uneasy feeling that something is going on out there.'

Just at that moment Bess began to growl down in the kitchen, much louder than on previous occasions when she had scented danger.

'Something has alarmed Bess,' Sabat muttered, 'maybe I'd better hang on a while before going up to bed. Rarely does that dog give a false alarm.'

'But there's nobody out there, you've just checked.' G. N. was puzzled too.

'When you're dealing with any aspect of the occult there's often something around that's not visible to the human eye.' Sabat continued to focus on the yard below them. 'Nothing that I can see... hey, hang on a minute!'

'What have you spotted?'

'Somebody creeping down the side of the sheep shed. Good God, it's that old farmer, Roberts!'

'But he came here last night. He'd got lost and you took him home. Surely to God he hasn't been roaming in the dark and lost his way again.'

'There is something decidedly fishy about this.' Sabat continued to focus on the slinking figure.

Bess's growls had reached a crescendo. Now she began to bark. Both men detected a trace of fear in her cries. A scratching of clawed feet noted that she had moved from beneath the table to the door. A warning?

'She didn't like Roberts on the last occasion, Mark. Now she's going crazy. Maybe we better go and see what he wants this time.'

'No. We'll stay here and watch. He won't know that I can see his every movement. He's heading this way but he clearly doesn't want to be seen. He's up to something.'

'But he's a frail old man. He can't harm us.'

'I've been in a lot of strange inexplicable situations throughout my career. I've learnt that it's dangerous to take anything at face value where the dark powers are concerned.'

'You surely don't think that he presents any danger?'

'Nothing would surprise me.'

Downstairs Bess was yelping. They heard the collie run back to the kitchen to her original hiding place. She continued to growl.

Sabat saw their visitor emerge from the shadows and revert to his stumbling gait as he neared the front door. That was when he experienced a strange sensation, akin to that over the years when Quentin's soul was rousing within him. No, not Quentin this time for his brother was gone from him at long last. It could only be the evil emanating from the Dark Powers which his acute sensitivity to its presence had picked up. He tensed, gripped the windowsill, drew a deep breath.

'What is it, Mark? What's wrong?'

'It's him down there, the farmer who calls himself Roberts. I picked up his vibes. I sensed something last time but now it's stronger than ever. *Take it from me, G. N., that's the Reaper down there!*'

'We'd better go down and...'

'No way. I don't know what his plan is, but we've had murder up there in the wood. That poacher died from Novichok and Sergeant Harrison is currently fighting for his life. Unless I miss my guess the Reaper's got a jet of it lined up for us.'

'Jesus Christ, what are we going to do? And where is Wilkes? He's surely seen the Reaper's approach but there's no sign of him.'

'Pray God I'm wrong, but the young copper wouldn't stand much chance against the most dangerous master criminal in this day and age.'

They heard footsteps coming across the landing and then Tony and Parnel appeared.

'What is it?' Parnel was clearly disturbed. 'Bess is

going crazy down in the kitchen.'

'We've got a visitor,' Sabat replied. 'Right now I'm expecting a knock on the door.'

'Who can it be in the middle of the night?'

'It's the guy who calls himself Roberts.'

'Why on earth…' Parnel broke off and pointed towards the window. 'Strewth, just look across there, the sky is lit up. There's a fire somewhere!?'

The four of them stared; saw the fiery glow which lit up the night sky.

'It's coming from somewhere over by Willow Field, the smallholding where Roberts lives. And yet he's here, creeping in on us. Has he set fire to his house before leaving it? Maybe he doesn't intend going back there. Once he's murdered us, he'll disappear. And has he killed PC Wilkes up beyond the barn?'

'Oh, my God!' Parnel clutched her hands together, an expression of panic on her face. 'What on earth are we going to do?'

At that moment there came a sharp rapping on the front door. Bess gave a loud whine of terror.

Sabat's fingers found the window catch. In his other hand he held his handgun at the ready. 'First of all,' he whispered to his companions, 'we'd better see what the so-called Mister Roberts has to say for himself. Move back just in case he decides to squirt some of that vile stuff up here.'

Down below in the yard, the man who called himself Victor Roberts was standing back from the door, both hands deep in his pockets. He looked up as he heard the creak of the window opening.

'May I come inside and talk to you?' The request was

in shaking tones, a note of desperation, pleading in them.

A short silence followed. Sabat drew a deep breath. 'It is rather late for you to be wandering about in the countryside, Mister Roberts.'

'My apologies for disturbing you at this hour,' the other had his back towards them now and with a shaking arm pointed to the fiery sky in the distance. 'There's... there's a fire. A big one, and I don't have a phone with which to call the brigade.'

'Your place?'

'Yes.' The Reaper knew only too well that it was Willow Field that was blazing. Those Russians had torched it before they did a runner. It figured. He had deprived them of the Roundhead treasure and they knew he would not return to pay them. An act of revenge; by now they would surely have left. He would not see them again.

'You must have passed the police guard at the murder scene on your way here. Why didn't you get them to phone the brigade?'

Sabat glanced at G. N. This situation was becoming more sinister by the minute.

'I came by a roundabout route. That area is cordoned off. I did not wish to come into contact with any of that Novichok stuff.'

Sabat's suspicions increased. How would Roberts know about the Novichok? Clearly all he wanted was for them to come downstairs and open the door. What then?

'If you would be so kind as to take me home,' their visitor's voice was scarcely audible. 'That fire over there,

I'm concerned in case Willow Field might be burning.'

'We'll be down shortly,' Sabat answered. 'We have to get dressed first. Give us a few minutes.'

'Thank you, I'll wait for you.'

The Reaper fingered the deadly spray gun in his pocket. For once, his hand was trembling. At long last the day of reckoning had arrived.

16

Two fire engines had arrived at Willow Field, followed by a police car and an ambulance. The crew unrolled their house, there was a convenient brook nearby which would supply all the water they needed.

'My God, what a blaze!' The chief fire officer commented as jets of water were directed onto the burning, decrepit farmhouse.

'There could be somebody inside,' one of the medics from the ambulance joined him.

'If there is then there's no chance of them still being alive. We'll have to wait until we put this lot out, and that won't be for a few hours yet.'

Just then the roof collapsed in a shower of sparks.

'Too much dry and woodworm eaten old timber in these old farm cottages,' the fireman shook his head. 'A log rolls out of an open fire and hey presto there's an inferno within minutes, and if the occupants happened to be asleep upstairs then they've got no chance. Or arson. That hill fire last summer was definitely started deliberately.'

'And a Novichok murder up there,' a constable indicated to the wooded hillside opposite. 'We heard before we were called out that Harrison has shown slight signs of improvement, he might just make it. They reckon the Reaper is around this area. Maybe he started this blaze for some reason but I can't figure out why he would want to kill a decrepit old farmer.'

'Once we can get this inferno doused we will search the place and maybe a mystery will be solved. It will be hours yet, though.'

Dawn was just starting to show in the eastern sky before the fire was doused, leaving a steaming heap of rubble amidst the remnants of the walls which still stood precariously.

'Right chaps,' Superintendent Baschurch addressed the four officers who had accompanied him. 'Just a cursory exploration at this stage to check if there are any bodies inside. Then we'll summon contractors to remove the rubble so that we can carry out a thorough search for clues.'

Using long handled rakes three of the police officers began their search, scraping ash and debris aside in order to afford entrance and a route through the remnants of the kitchen.

'There's a cellar down there,' one of the searchers indicated the remains of a fire devastated wooden door with stone steps leading down beyond it. 'It seems to have escaped the worst of the blaze above.'

A powerful flashlight shone down into the cavity below.

'Christ, there's a couple of guys on the steps!' The

policeman coughed in the smoky atmosphere. 'They're dead, all right. The ones got his ankle bound up and… oh, *my God, look over there…A kind of upside-down altar and there's… there's another corpse there, all cut up!'* That was when he vomited.

'Move away!' His companion shouted and began to retreat. 'There's been Novichock used on that murder up in the wood, it might be around here, too.'

Panicking, the officers ploughed their way back through the ash and debris then stumbled out into the open.

'What the hell is up with you?' Baschurch growled.

'Never seen anything like it,' came the breathless reply. 'There's dead bodies inside, down in the cellar. You won't believe this but there's some sort of altar with an upturned cross and… there's another corpse lying in front of it… all cut to pieces like it's been…sacrificed!'

For a moment the superintendent was too stunned to reply, then 'I'll get word to the unit up there in the wood they can summon the counter-terrorist guys who responded to the initial call. Let them remove the bodies, cordon this place off.' He wiped his sweaty brow.

'Right,' he addressed the gathering of police officers, firemen and paramedics waiting beside the ambulance. 'Everybody stand well clear of this property. Williams, Jackson, erect a cordon around the front entrance and ensure that nobody goes beyond it. That damned nerve agent might just be a factor here like it was up there in the wood. We can't take any chances.'

The others moved to obey their chief's orders. Baschurch wiped his sweating brow. Whatever next? He had an uneasy feeling that these terrible events were far from over.

17

'I'm convinced that Roberts is none other than the Reaper,' Sabat's expression was grim. 'My hunches have never failed me in all the years I have been working as an occult investigator. He's got some evil plan. Just what we're going to do right now I don't have any idea. He wants revenge on you G. N., but exactly how I don't know. He might plan to shoot you the moment we open the door or...'

'Or what?'

'Novichok was used to murder that poacher up in the wood and we know what happened to Sergeant Harrison. He got a secondary dose of it. It's the most dangerous nerve agent in existence. We can't chance coming into contact with it.'

'I could shoot him from here,' his companion replied, 'like I almost did that time before, except that inexplicably a roaming wolf took the bullet.'

'But just suppose that Roberts isn't the Reaper,' Mark shook his head. 'Then you would face a charge of murder. For once, I just don't know how to handle this. And apart from ourselves the girls are at risk. No doubt he would murder them as well.'

Down below, Bess was howling. There was no mistaking her fear. In her own way she was warning the occupants of the house.

The tapping on the door had increased to a loud banging. Their visitor was becoming impatient.

'Open up!' A shout.

'No way,' Sabat breathed, 'none of us are opening that door.'

'Then what's the next move? Do we sit here all night and hope that he'll go away? Which he won't, if he *is* the Reaper.'

An uneasy silence followed, broken by the appearance of Parnel and Toni.

'There's somebody at the door,' Parnel had a strained expression on her face. 'They're hammering away and Bess is going crazy.'

'It's...' Sabat's reply was drowned by a loud howl, followed by a chorus which shattered the stillness of the night outside.

'It's those wolves again!' He half rose and focused his night vision optic. 'They're close, just beyond the far barn I'd say. Can't see anything... yes, I can now, a trio of them!'

'Then where's Wilkes?'

'The wolves moved out into the open yard. The one leading them, stretched its neck and let out a long howl.

'There must be others following,' Mark Sabat grunted, 'and he's summoning them to join him. There, up there, by the field gate. Three more. The others appear to be waiting for them to join them. As I told you, G. N., a bunch of them means they are hunting large prey. There are sheep on the hillside but they haven't touched them. They're headed down here; sensed something.'

'Wilkes?'

'Then why doesn't he open fire on those that passed the end shed?'

'That's what worries me.'

There came another frantic hammering on the door followed by a cry. 'Let me in. There's wolves out here!'

'That isn't Roberts' voice,' Sabat stiffened. 'It's not the shaky, grating voice of an old man. Roberts is the Reaper, all right, and in his fear he's forgotten to continue with his old man act.'

A shot rang out from down below. The leading wolf stumbled, but somehow regained its balance. A second report. This time it fell and rolled over kicking. Its companions had bunched, snarling.

They stood at bay. Victor Roberts had backed up against the wall. Three more wolves appeared at the far end of the yard, holding back from the gunfire.

'Jesus,' Sabat breathed. 'I thought the bugger could summon the wolves at will, bestial companions answering his command. Not this time it seems. *They're after him!'*

Another couple of shots rang out, aimed at the distant beasts. They stood their ground, then howled mournfully as though they were calling upon some supernatural power to protect them.

Bess's growling had changed to a whine, for some unknown reason she was no longer afraid.

Parnell and Toni had joined the menfolk at the window, staring in disbelief at the scene below.

Another shot rang out from the Reaper's handgun. The wolves stood their ground. Waiting, as though they sensed a climax was imminent.

A series of clicks rang in the still atmosphere.

'His gun's empty!' Sabat muttered. 'What now?'

That was when the watching wolves seemed to sense that for the moment no danger threatened them. The distant ones moved forward to join their companions below. They hunched, snarling ferociously.

The Reaper was attempting to reload. Maybe for the first time in his life he was panicking, fumbling. Live and spent shells clinked on the ground.

That was when the wolves charged; a frenzied howling rush, jaws wide. They sensed that their intended prey was no longer a threat to them.

'Master!' The Reaper screamed, a desperate plea to the Dark One whom he had served faithfully over the years.

Then the rabid beasts were upon him, knocking him down, greedily tearing at any exposed skin. The flesh from a cheek was ripped away, exposing bone that turned scarlet as the blood flowed.

A wolf which was barely more than a cub tore a ribbon of meat that trailed; chewed it with a soft crunching sound at a distance from the others.

Others were frantically ripping clothing away from the body in their desperation to expose the flesh beneath. Somehow their human victim still lived, his cries of pain and fear reduced to a series of barely audible whines.

The hand of his remaining arm delved inside his ribboned coat and closed over the hilt of the knife which was in a sheath strapped around his torso. Huge teeth scraped on the long blade. They jerked it clear as though the beasts knew that it presented a threat. It clanged and clattered on the ground.

That same hand sought and found a pocket in the shredded coat which somehow clung to the victim's body. Delving deep, finding what it sought, a lightweight plastic cylinder. Novichock was Joseph Palmer's last desperate hope. One jet sprayed over the snarling furry mass of his attackers would destroy them; they would share his agony in their death throes.

Then, just as he gripped his most deadly weapon, the hand which grasped at it was torn from his wrist, blood spouting from the severed artery.

A scream that was little more than a barely audible groan. Even in the throes of his final agony he heard the cylinder bouncing away, rolling clear of the bloody melee.

That was when he finally gave up all hope of survival, every orifice in his body bleeding profusely, crimson rivulets which wolven tongues licked greedily as they bit and tore at human meat.

Up above, both women had turned away. They could no longer bear to look upon the scene below them.

'It's...awful,' Parnel thought that she might throw up.

'Except that it's the Reaper down there,' G. N. could not resist gloating. 'Think of the bodies he's mutilated in his vile sacrifices to his Master; torture and murder on an unprecedented scale. Don't feel sorry for him, the wolves are doing to him what he's done to others, and us a favour.'

The ravening beasts fed greedily on human flesh, bones snapping with loud cracks. They had eaten between his splayed legs, the softest, most succulent meat of all, bloodied jaws munching, succulent flesh stringing from them.

They began to quarrel over their prey, snapping at their companions even though there was enough for them all to feast on; torn garments in all directions, blood soaked.

'*God Almighty*!' Sabat turned away, even he was revolted by the savage carnage.

'Do we shoot them?' G. N. asked, the Drilling poised, a 9.3×87 shell loaded and ready to fire.

'No,' his companion shook his head. 'Let them feed, make sure that the Reaper is finished once and for all. We'll wait for daylight and hopefully those wolves will have gone back to wherever they came from. Then I'll call the police, get a unit to clear up the mess and well see where we go from there.'

Parnel and Toni returned to their beds. Sabat and G. N. sat in silence listening to the feeding wolves, their gnawing and snapping at one another in their greed for this unprecedented meal.

Down in the kitchen Bess had fallen silent, almost as though she was accepting the happenings outside, relieved that it was all over and that their terrible visitor was no more.

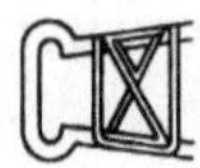

The night hours seemed endless to the occupants of Chestnut Farm. Then, finally, the eastern sky began to lighten with the coming of dawn.

Daylight came quickly, exposing every inch of the farmyard below, the bloody morass and shredded garments that had once been Joseph Palmer, the Reaper. There was no sign of the wolves other than the one which lay dead, killed by the Reaper's handgun before the others had pulled him down.

'I guess we'd better go and take a look around, see what's happened to PC Wilkes,' Mark Sabbat struggled to throw off the weariness which engulfed him. Both he and G. N. dreaded what they might find out there.

Parnel and Toni were sleeping in bed, exhausted by the events of the night hours. G. N. had the loaded Drilling beneath his arm, Sabat held his revolver in his right hand. His left hand fingered the crucifix which was suspended from his neck. Both were prepared for anything which they might encounter outside.

'My God!' G. N. stared at the remains of the Reaper, the bile rising in his throat. 'Hey, what's that over there? It looks like a kid's water pistol.'

'I guess it's loaded with Novichock,' Sabat's extended arm restrained the other. 'Don't go anywhere near it. In all probability he never got a chance to use it, otherwise we'd have seen those wolves writing in agony. All the same we'll give it a wide berth, leave it to the experts to retrieve. You know what happened to Sergeant Harrison.'

At the far end of the outbuildings, hidden from view from their lookout position they found PC Wilkes. His gashed and open bloody throat was frozen in his final scream.

'As I suspected,' Sabat shook his head, 'murdered by the Reaper. God, I hope that bastard really suffered at the end.'

Rarely was Mark Sabat visibly shaken, he had witnessed many gruesome scenes throughout his long career. This was somehow different because all that had happened in the build up to the violent death at Chestnut Farm.

'I…' suddenly Sabat pointed to a grass covered bank beyond. 'My God, look there… *it's that adder again!*'

'Where? I can't see anything?'

'It's disappeared, like it did the last time, there one second, gone the next!'

Both men rushed over to where the viper had been. The grass was short, there was no place where it could have wriggled out of sight.'

'I... I just don't understand it,' Mark shook his head in disbelief. 'First it was up in the priest hole, then when I caught it and dumped it up here it just vanished like it had never existed. Now it's happened again!'

'It's...it's unbelievable,' G. N. was clearly shaken.

'Seems for once I read the signs wrong,' Sabat pursed his lips. 'That adder was not evil, it appeared as a warning to us and I ignored it. Well, we'd better get back to the house and I'll summon the police, get this dreadful mess cleared up. The Reaper is no more. My job here is finished.'

18

Mark, G. N., Toni and Purnel had moved temporarily to G. N.'s cottage whilst a thorough investigation and decontamination process had been carried out at Chestnut Farm. Having found the Novichok spray, the authorities were taking no chances of any of the nerve agent being present there.

A few days later they received a visit from Superintendent Baschurch.

'I'm pleased to inform you that Chestnut Farm has been completely decontaminated,' the latter's relief was evident. 'None of the liquid had escaped from the container which the Reaper had had in his possession. There was not much left of his corpse,' he grimaced, 'but we have proved beyond all doubt that it was Joseph Palmer. An exceedingly clever disguise incorporating a skin graft.'

'How is Sergeant Harrison?' Sabat voiced the question which had been on their minds for the past few days.

'He's making an excellent recovery,' Baschurch smiled. 'In fact, he's likely to be discharged from the hospital in a week or so. Needless to say, he won't be back at work for some time.'

'What about the fire at Willow Field?' Sabat raised another question.

'Ah,' the officer shook his head. 'That is where the mystery lies, and I doubt if it will ever be satisfactorily solved. There were three bodies down in the cellar, all of them unharmed by the fire which raged above.'

'My God!' Sabat was taken aback. What the hell had been going on that night? 'Who on earth were the corpses?'

'One was that missing youth, Ricky Brown. He had been sacrificed before an upturned altar. Black magic, I guess, symptomatic of the Reaper's supposed connection with the dark forces.'

G. N. grimaced.

'Who were the others?' Sabat asked.

'A couple of Russians, we've managed to identify them, their vehicle was parked up on the cattle market car park, obviously handy for a quick departure after their mission was completed. Their names were Osmakcic and Dimitri, living in Britain as part of a spy exchange with Russia a few years ago. Prior to their move up here they were based in Bristol. We believe that they could have been connected with the Novichok poisonings in Salisbury and Amesbury, together with the pair identified and now back in Russia, but it will probably never be proved.'

'How come they were assisting the Reaper?'

'We can only hazard a guess at that. Since the

Reaper's incarceration his criminal network in Europe became part of the Pink Panther organisation. He was still involved and there is a possibility that this pair of Russians were brought in to assist him. A very convenient arrangement. Investigations are still ongoing.'

'How did they die?' Sabat asked.

'They had been squirting Novichock, God knows what at. It was all over that satanic altar, or whatever it was. Needless to say, they came into contact with it. I don't need to tell you about the agony they must have suffered before they died. Along with smoke inhalation from the fire upstairs. There is one strange factor, though, which is puzzling.'

'What's that?'

The guy named Osmakcic had an adder bite on his ankle. It was bound up, but the infection had spread. Without treatment he might have died anyway.'

'Strewth!' Sabat was taken aback.

'What's so amazing about that?' Baschurch raised his eyebrows. 'There's adders about in this part of the countryside. He could have gone outside for a breath of fresh air, got bitten. I don't think it's relevant to everything else that happened. He didn't go to the hospital for his presence in this area might be revealed.'

'Well, the adder certainly wasn't evil towards us,' Sabat remarked after Baschurch had departed. 'It wasn't sent by the Reaper's Master. It was here to warn us. For some inexplicable reason the Dark Powers deserted him at the end. We'll never know why. Those wolves even turned on him, destroyed him. Whatever, we should be grateful. They saved our lives.'

'We'll be leaving for Aberdeen, tomorrow,' Mark announced over supper. All four of them had moved back into Chestnut Farm. It seemed that G. N. would be living here from now on. A relationship appeared to have developed between him and Parnel, but neither of them mentioned it.

'Toni and I are planning to marry,' Sabat continued.

A silence greeted his announcement.

'And he's actually going to retire,' Toni stated. 'No more weird investigations. I shall see to that personally.'

The others smiled. Sabat nodded his assent. It was an attractive prospect. *If* it really worked out. He had an uneasy feeling that there would be a next time. Only time would tell.

ABOUT THE AUTHOR

Guy N. Smith has been a best-selling author for over 40 years. He has published 120 novels and around 400 short stories and articles on various subjects.

Night of the Crabs became an instant best seller with the movie rights sold. Since then there have been no fewer than 7 sequels. *Killer Crabs* is currently being filmed.

Find out more at www.guynsmith.com

Guy N. Smith's
Werewolf Omnibus

Are werewolves simply folklore or have they existed at some stage in the distant past?

Lycanthropy is known to be a mental condition where the sufferer believes himself to be a wolf and embarks upon a psychotic rampage. So perhaps there's some truth in the age-old legends.

The Black Hill in South Shropshire is a dark forest where legend becomes reality. As well as werewolves seeking human prey, the hills hold tales of the black dogs. A sighting of these spectral canines is a harbinger of death.

Gordon Hall, the sporting tenant, finds himself caught up in these ancient horrors and is determined to destroy them once and for all.

Both his life and his soul are at risk.

Werewolf Omnibus collects together three vintage novels from the master of pulp horror, Guy N. Smith: Werewolf By Moonlight (1974), Return Of The Werewolf (1977) and The Son Of The Werewolf (1978), alongside a new short story, Spawn Of The Werewolf.

HORROR LURKED IN THE MAZE OF CLIFF CAVES WHERE A
NEW GENERATION OF GIANT CRABS WERE BREEDING.
THE CHARNEL CAVES
GUY N. SMITH

The Charnel Caves: A Crabs Novel

Horror lurked in the maze of cliff caves where a new generation of giant crabs were breeding.

In 1975 an army of gigantic crabs, the result of an underwater nuclear experiment, attacked the Welsh coastline.

The battle was bloody, many lives were lost until the crustacean invaders were defeated.

Over the ensuing years they turned up in the oceans of the World with further terrible slaughter of humans. Finally, though, it was believed that these monsters from the deep had been eradicated. Only memories of their invasions of land remained with the older inhabitants, tales of their depredations on mankind were whispered but often ridiculed by the modern generations.

Until a few of the survivors returned to the Welsh coast and began breeding secretly in a maze of caverns beneath the cliffs, preparing for a further attack on mankind.

The Black Room Manuscripts Volume Three

Guy N. Smith features in *The Black Room Manuscripts Volume Three* with his short story **Toad In The Hole**.

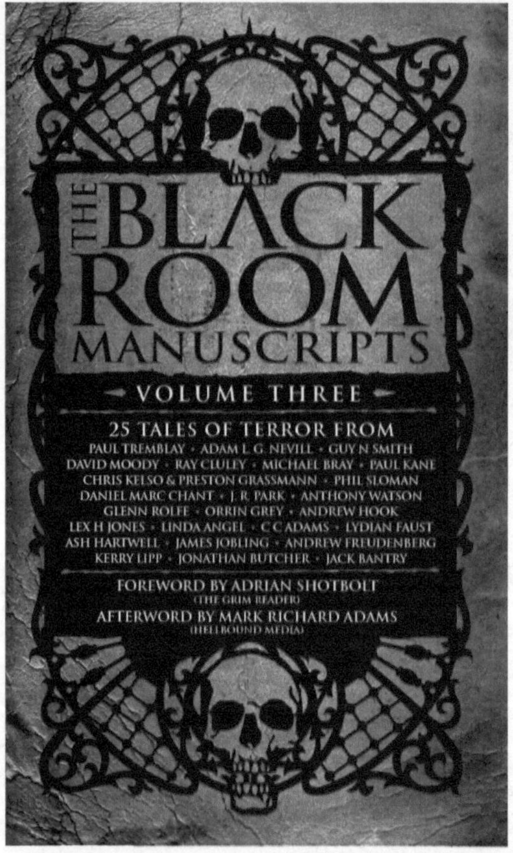

All profits made the sale of this book go to the charity Shelter.

The Black Room Manuscripts Volume Three

Some words are born in shadows.

Some tales told only in whispers.

Under the paper thin veneer of our sanity is a world that exists. Hidden just beyond, in plain sight, waiting to consume you should you dare stray from the street-lit paths that sedate our fears.
For centuries the Black Room has stored stories of these encounters, suppressing the knowledge of the rarely seen. Protecting the civilised world from its own dark realities.
The door to the Black Room has once again swung open to unleash twenty five masterful tales of the macabre from the twisted minds of a new breed of horror author.

The Black Room holds many secrets.

Dare you enter…for a third time?

"The sheer effort and dedication that's gone into creating this unbelievably comprehensive bibliography is breath-taking." – DLS Reviews

The complete(ish) guide to collecting the works of Guy N. Smith.

A journey into collecting the works of prolific author Guy Newman Smith. The book covers all genres of the Great Scribbler's writing and contains over 950 pictures and useful details to assist any would-be collector.

Guy N. Smith Illustrated Bibliography

The author has endeavoured to list and visually represent, through over 950 colour pictures, the vast catalogue of output from Guy N. Smith's 65+ years in print; from the early stories he had published in the Tettenhall Observer and Advertiser paper as a teenager through to the present day. A career that crosses fiction and non-fiction and has covered almost all possible genres along the way, from Self-Sufficiency to Westerns, via Countryside and Glamour magazines of the 70s, all in addition to the numerous horror and thriller titles he is better known for.

Content includes Fiction (all imprints/editions inc. non UK) and Non-Fiction Categories: Horror, Thriller, Countryside and Children's Novels, Omnibus Collections, Chapbooks, Graphic Novels, Anthologies, Fanzines, Booklets, Magazines (70s adult Glamour, Country Sport, Game-keeping, Horror etc.), Periodicals and Newspapers.

The book also contains an original Guy N. Smith short story 'The Beast in the Cage' along with humorous insight into the levels of collecting Guy N. Smith's works in 'The Completist- A Cautionary Tale' by author Shane P.D Agnew.

A4 Size, 950+ colour pictures, 341 pages.

Available via Amazon.

The Sinister Horror Company is an independent UK publisher of genre fiction. Their mission a simple one – to write, publish and launch innovative and exciting genre fiction by themselves and others.

For further information on the Sinister Horror Company visit:

SinisterHorrorCompany.com
Facebook.com/sinisterhorrorcompany
Twitter @SinisterHC

SINISTERHORRORCOMPANY.COM